The Re the Rectory

Viola Roberts Cozy Mystery
Book 6

Shéa MacLeod

Shéa MacLeod

The Remains in the Rectory
Viola Roberts Cozy Mystery Book 6
Text copyright © 2017 Shéa MacLeod
All rights reserved.
Printed in the United States of America.

Cover design by Mariah Sinclair/mariahsinclair.com
Editing by Yvette Keller
Formatted by PyperPress

The characters and events portrayed in this book are fictitious. Any similarity to real persons, living or dead, is coincidental and not intended by the author.

No part of this book may be reproduced, or stored in a retrieval system, or transmitted in any form or by any means, electronic, mechanical, photocopying, recording, or otherwise, without express written permission of the publisher.

The Remains in the Rectory

DEDICATION

For all my lovely friends in England
who embraced me as one of their own.

Chapter 1
Lost in Translation

Driving on the wrong side of the road is not something I'd recommend. Especially if you want to keep both your sanity and your relationship intact.

"Watch the hedgerow, Viola!" Lucas braced himself against the dashboard of the ridiculously small Peugeot, knuckles turning white as I took the curve a little too fast. The hedgerow loomed ominously close.

"Shut up," I snapped. "I'm trying to drive, here." I'd been driving nearly thirty years, after all. I should be getting the hang of it by now.

Whose idea was this, anyway? Renting a car in England. Driving out to the picturesque Cotswolds. It had all sounded so great until the realities of driving on the left set in and I nearly sideswiped a lorry. (An American would have said truck, not lorry, but I was trying really hard to get into the spirit of the thing. It wasn't my fault, really. Left hand driving just doesn't come naturally to a person.

My boyfriend, Lucas Salvatore, sat hunched in the passenger's seat of the small rental car, alternately cussing and praying. Lucas was a few years older than me, making him closer to fifty than forty. He was ridiculously handsome with his bronzed skin and dark hair lightly peppered with gray. Usually he was a calm and supportive partner, but frankly, he was getting on my last nerve. I was perfectly capable of figuring this driving thing out without killing us. Probably.

We were somewhere out on what the English refer to as a "B road." In the States, it would be a country lane: narrow, harrowing. Filled with tractors and the distinct possibility of ending up with a deer in your windshield. Or rather, since this was England, a sheep.

Lucas and I were both writers. He wrote best-selling thrillers which Hollywood eagerly turned into blockbuster movies starring that actor with the big nose. I wrote western historical romances with cowboys and mail order brides. I made an excellent living, but Hollywood wasn't knocking.

When Lucas had suggested attending the London Book Fair, I'd jumped at the chance to leave my sodden little town of Astoria, Oregon for the wildly exotic (and equally sodden) streets of London. Our plan after the fair was to tour the English countryside by car. Lucas wanted to find some unexplored English village to include in his latest novel. So that's how we found ourselves on a B road, out in the Cotswolds, with Lucas snippy, me snappy, and lorries trying to murder us.

"How far have we got to go?" I said between gritted teeth. My smartphone wasn't working even though the carrier had promised it would, and the GPS system had crapped out thirty minutes ago.

Lucas battled with a paper map for a minute. "A couple more miles and we'll hit the turn off to the Roman

Road. Then it's a straight shot to Moreton-in-Marsh. We can get the A44 to Oxford from there."

Oxford. And civilization! I could hardly wait. Just a little farther and we'd be back on "A roads" with properly definitely lanes. I breathed a sigh of relief.

And then the skies, which had been dark and ominous all day, suddenly opened up and dumped rain on us. It was like a freaking monsoon. I turned the wiper blades on high, and still I could barely make out the road ahead. My hands ached from gripping the steering wheel so tight.

"There's a branch in the road up here somewhere," Lucas said. "Keep right."

I nodded, but didn't take my eyes off the road, even though at this point I could barely see it. The only thing keeping me out of the ditch was the hedgerow looming to my left, so close the occasional branch scraped the side of the car. I sure hoped Lucas bought extra insurance to cover the scratches. If not, it would be a good reminder for him not to bother me while driving in a country influenced by Romans. It was thanks to them that the entire country insisted on driving on the wrong side of the road. I suppose one didn't want to block one's sword arm. Because I'd seen so many sword-carrying Audi drivers.

We drove three more miles before I said, "Where's that fork we were supposed to take?"

Lucas shrugged. "We should have found it by now, but maybe it's further up?"

I kept going, a sick feeling in my stomach. There were no signs indicating where we were or how close the next town was. I could only see a few inches in front of the windshield. I was starting to think we'd be lost out here forever, wandering in the English wilderness.

"Stop being dramatic."

I slid my gaze toward Lucas who was shaking his head. I frowned. "I didn't say anything."

"No. But you were thinking it." His voice was lightly accented with a rumbly sexiness to it.

I pointedly ignored him. "We're low on gas."

"Petrol," he corrected in an annoying fashion. "Once we get out on the Roman Road we should be okay."

"If we can find the cursed thing," I muttered.

The Roman Road was exactly what it sounded like: an ancient road built by the Romans which had been paved over a few decades back and turned into an A road. It was straight as an arrow—more or less—rising up hills and falling down dales. It marched its way across the landscape, much like its builders had, once upon a time. Unfortunately, it was nowhere in sight and I was stuck winding around the narrow backroad feeling lost and claustrophobic with the hedgerows pressing in on either side.

I knew it was dumb, but I was desperate to get off the B road as soon as possible. So, I said the Lord's Prayer that the tractors were all at home avoiding the rain, and pressed down on the gas pedal. The car lurched as it sped up.

"There!" Lucas shouted, jabbing a finger to the right. Sure enough, an even narrower road led off to the right. I jerked the steering wheel hard and hit the road at full tilt. It bounced and jarred something awful, until I was able to slow down enough to not kill us.

"That wasn't exactly a fork," I pointed out.

"True," he admitted, "but it was the first gap I saw in that abominable hedgerow. This has to be the road. There's been nothing else."

I wasn't so sure. The rain was pouring buckets. Every now and then the tires made a desperate attempt to hydroplane. Fortunately, I'm from a state where it rains more often than not. This was a piece of cake for me. If the cake was full of nuts and lumps of baking soda.

The narrow lane—it could hardly be described as a road—wound its way through a copse of trees, around thickets of brush, across a stone bridge, and past fields of some kind or other. Green shoots stood stubbornly beneath the onslaught of rain. Up ahead I saw a figure swathed in a yellow rain slicker slogging alongside the road. He, or she, wore rubber boots of ordinary green and had the slicker hood up. One hand gripped a gnarled walking stick, though it seemed to be more for effect than out of necessity.

"Pull up alongside," Lucas urged. "Surely this person can give us directions."

I did as instructed and Lucas rolled down the window. "Pardon me!" His usually faint accent grew suddenly thicker and sounded more British than it usually did. It didn't escape my notice that he also used British phrasing instead of American, as he did back home.

The figure in the slicker stopped and turned to face us. Although the face was rough, wrinkled, and devoid of makeup, it was still of the feminine variety.

"What are you two doing way out here?" The accent was thick with the slightly nasal intonations of the Midlands. The voice itself was strong and low, but definitely female. "You get yourselves lost?"

"Something like that," Lucas said. I couldn't see his face, but I knew he was giving the woman his most charming smile. "We're trying to find the Roman Road."

"Oh, that's way back there." She waved vaguely in the direction we'd come. So we *had* missed the fork. Darn it. "Some two, three miles."

"Well, that's no good. We're low on petrol, you see. Is there a village ahead?" he asked.

"Oh, ay. There is that." She gave him a warm smile, but no further information. I felt like smacking the wheel in frustration, but Lucas remained his calm, charming self. Naturally.

"How far is it? Do you think?"

She squinted off into the rain, the lines around her eyes feathering out. "'Bout a mile, I'd say. Give or take."

"Well, that's perfect." Lucas flashed his pearly whites. "Is there a turn off or anything?"

"Just keep on this road and you'll come to it. Can't miss it."

"Can we give you a ride?" he asked.

I scowled at him, though he couldn't see. I did not need her dripping water all over the rental car. I could just see trying to explain mildew stains on top of the paint scratches.

"Thank you, no. Got to get my walk in, you see."

"Of course. Thank you."

She nodded as Lucas rolled the window up and I put the car back in "drive." I frowned at the gas gauge. I sure hoped we had enough gas for a mile "or so." The gas light had been on for some time.

Just as the engine started sputtering, we rolled out of the woods and into a village. A small sign, impossible to read in the downpour, marked the outskirts. Such as they were. Stone buildings stood sentinel on either side of the narrow lane, blurred by rain, leaning against each other as if for support against the storm.

"We're not getting much further and I don't see a gas station," I said.

"Petrol station. It's fine. There's a pub. Pull in there."

Sure enough, there was one of those half-timbered old buildings with a sign swinging out front and lights burning brightly. A small parking lot to the side could hold about three cars. And lucky us, there was a spot empty. I pulled in just as the engine finally died.

Lucas grinned. "Perfect timing."

I glared at him. "If we hadn't gotten lost, it would have been fine."

"And whose fault is it we got lost?"

"Well," I said with a glare. "You were the navigator."

"Come on, Viola," he laughed. "This is an adventure. Let's see where it takes us." He climbed out of the car cutting off any reply I might have made.

With a sigh I climbed out, too, ducking my head against the onslaught of wind and rain. Lucas grabbed my hand and we ran to the pub side by side. Lucas stopped to jerk open the door and we hurried out of the cold and into the warm, steamy building.

To my left was an old, stone fireplace where flames danced cheerfully, casting a cozy glow into the room. Ahead and slightly to the right was a scarred wooden bar with the standard liquor bottles and glasses clustered on shelves behind it. The ceiling was low, heavy beams dark with age, and the floor flagstone, worn smooth by hundreds of feet. Around the room clustered comfy chairs, perfect for relaxing with a drink. There were small groupings of proper tables and chairs for more easily eating whatever heavenly smelling delicacy was currently cooking in the kitchen. According to the chalkboard, the daily specials were fish and chips and sausage and mash.

The pub was small, but chock full of ambience. A man who looked about a hundred perched on a stool, his newsboy cap pulled low over his forehead. He hunched over his half-empty pint of beer. Two couples were gathered near the window—not that they could see much in this storm—sharing a meal and talking in low voices. Otherwise the place was empty. No one looked up when we entered which I found very odd.

"Why don't we sit near the fire," Lucas suggested. "Warm ourselves up."

I shrugged. "Sure. I could dry out."

I sank into one of the twin leather chairs next to the fire. On the small occasional table between them was a menu. The cover carried the name of the pub: Beast and Bauble. They did love their wacky names around here.

"Anything to drink?" Lucas asked as he draped his jacket over the back of the other chair.

"Blackberry bourbon, of course."

He smiled. "Of course. But I've a feeling they might not have it."

I sighed. "Fine. Baileys and coffee. Heavy on the Baileys." I might be driving, but I wasn't going anywhere at the moment and neither was the car.

Lucas collected our drinks from the bartender and settled in. "This is perfect." A dreamy smile curved his full lips.

I eyed him narrowly. "What's perfect?"

"This village. This pub. Don't you feel it? The atmosphere?"

Usually I was the one waxing poetic about things. This turn of events made me uneasy. "You want to research *this* village for your novel?"

"Why not?" He took a sip of his drink.

"We haven't even seen the place. It might be awful."

He grinned, gray eyes twinkling. "Oh, I've a good feeling."

"Great," I muttered around my coffee. "Now he's getting feelings."

Lucas merely chuckled.

The old man turned on his stool and eyeballed us mournfully. "Don't get many visitors," he said. "Welcome to Chipping Poggs." He raised his half-empty pint glass and then slugged back a good swallow.

"Thanks," Lucas and I chimed before taking more genteel sips of our own drinks.

Chipping Poggs? What a name. I exchanged a glance with Lucas who looked more excited than ever.

"Told you so," he muttered.

"Simon Briggs. What brings you folks this way?" the old man asked, wiping his mouth on his sleeve. I noticed thickets of white hair sprouting out his ears and down his nostrils and wondered vaguely if he had any left on his head.

"I'm Viola Roberts and this is my boyfriend, Lucas Salvatore," I said. "Is there a petrol station in town?" I wasn't about to admit we were searching for a village with "atmosphere" for my boyfriend's next book.

"'Fraid not. Closest one be about half-way between here and Chipping Camden."

"We're a bit lost," Lucas admitted. "We were trying to get back to Oxford for the night, but we must've taken a wrong turn somewhere."

"Oh, aye, that you did. But not to worry. We've got a lovely inn here in town."

"I didn't see one on the way in," I said. Granted, it had been pouring down rain so I couldn't see much of anything, but there definitely hadn't been anything that appeared inn-like.

"You wouldn't," Simon said. "It's on the other side of town." He waved vaguely. "Up at the old manor house. The family couldn't afford the upkeep, so they turned it into an inn. Very popular with tourists and whatnot. And at least it's not as haunted as the church." He waggled his bushy eyebrows, clearly hoping to pique our interest. He did not hope in vain.

"You have a haunted church? Is that even possible?" I asked.

"Oh, aye." His eyes twinkled, obviously realizing he had a captive audience. "Let me tell you about the ghosts of Chipping Poggs."

Shéa MacLeod

Chapter 2
The Ghosts of Chipping Poggs

"It were ten years ago this month," Simon Briggs began, leaning back on his stool until it creaked and groaned under his slight weight. He eyed the low-beamed ceiling as if to gather inspiration. "A stormy night just like this one."

Thunder crashed, emphasizing the fierceness of the weather. I jumped a little and shot Lucas a glare when he chuckled. Could I help it if thunder wasn't my favorite sound in the world? I settled back into my cozy chair, the warm mug comforting in my hands. "Go on."

Simon took a sip of his beer. "Old Mrs. Tillicum was out walking her dog when she saw the most terrifying sight."

Lucas leaned forward eagerly. "What was it?"

"The ghost of Mattie Doon wandering the churchyard. Near scared a year's life off her, it did. She ran home, locked herself in, and swore she'd never enter the church again."

"I think you need to back up a bit," Lucas said, crossing one jean clad leg over the other.

Simon peered at him over the rim of his pint. His eyebrows edged together to form one, long, caterpillar-like line of confusion. "Beg pardon?"

"Who is, or was, Mattie Doon?"

Simon frowned. "Didn't I say that part?"

"No," I said gently. "You started with Mrs. Tillicum and her dog."

Simon's brow unfurrowed. "Oh, well. No wonder you're confused!" He slapped his knee and chortled as if it were the funniest thing ever. I took a deep, fortifying gulp of my rapidly cooling Irish coffee. I had a feeling I would need it. Was the man mad? Or just forgetful?

"Why don't you start with the Baron, Simon?" The bartender leaned his beefy forearms against the bar. He was a short, thick man, nearly bald and of indiscriminate age. His sleeves were rolled up to reveal an anchor tattoo and a lot of wild, springy arm hair. I put him anywhere between forty-five and sixty-five. He was nursing his own pint of dark liquid. Was that even legal? Then again, who was going to bother arresting him? We were in the middle of nowhere.

"Right. Right. The Baron." Simon squinted into the distance. "Let's see, back about a hundred years or so..."

"More like two hundred," the bartender interrupted.

Simon shot him a sour look. "Fine. Two hundred. Baron Wytham was lord of Wytham Manor here in Chipping Poggs."

"The one that's an inn now?" I asked.

"Aye. That be the one," Simon assured me. "He was, what, the 16th Baron Wytham?"

"17th," the bartender supplied.

"Right. 17th Baron Wytham. Now, legend has it that the Baron Wytham was rather hard on his women. His first wife died in childbirth. Second got caught in a downpour and died of the fever—though there are those as claims he poisoned her. Third wife just up and disappeared one night. He claimed she run off with the gamekeeper, but no one saw them after that and he had her declared dead, so there's that."

"There's that, indeed," murmured Lucas.

I shot him a "shut up" look. This was getting juicy. My writer brain was already churning out ideas.

"In any case, the Baron was now in his sixty-fourth year and, if his portrait up at the manor is to be believed, was not a fortunate looking man. Mayhap that's why they called him 'Baron Pig.'"

"Nobody called him Baron Pig 'cept you," the bartender interrupted.

"Sure they did," Simon argued.

The bartender shook his head and set his pint aside. "If you say so." He grabbed a damp cloth and began wiping down the already pristine bar. "Go on if you must."

Simon ignored him. "Where was I?"

"The Baron was unfortunate looking and old," I said helpfully.

"Indeed. What a good memory you have, m'dear." I had a feeling he'd have patted my head if I was sitting close enough. "Now, in the village there was a maiden named Margaret Doon. Folks 'round here called her Mattie and she was young and beautiful as a newborn day." The man was waxing poetic and my drink was getting cold, but I was hooked. "The Baron set his eye on Mattie despite him being old enough to be her grandfather. And, as he was rich and a Baron, he forced Mattie into marrying him."

"Ew." I couldn't help myself. "The poor girl."

"Indeed. Indeed." Simon smacked his lips. His pint was empty.

"Let me get you another, Simon," Lucas offered, rising from his chair by the fire.

"Too kind," Simon said, beaming at Lucas. He handed over his glass and then carried on. "Mattie wasn't the weak willed type, however. She knew there was but one way to escape the Baron's clutches. So, the day of the wedding, she arrived early at the church and climbed to the bell tower. When the Baron and his entourage arrived, she appeared at the top of the tower and called to them. After placing a curse on the Baron, she threw herself to the courtyard below."

"Holy cannoli!" Even though I'd sort of known where this was going, it was still a shock. Especially with Simon giving such an emotive delivery. I leaned forward eagerly. "What sort of curse did she put on the Baron?"

"She said that he would not live to harm another woman. And he didn't. He died that night in the middle of trying to molest a maid at his manor house. Heart attack some said, but others claim it was the curse." His eyes twinkled with excitement. Clearly the man was a born storyteller.

"And the ghost?" I prompted as Lucas returned with Simon's drink.

"Thank you kindly, young man." Simon took a deep swallow. "Well, they say the ghost of Mattie Doon walks the churchyard to this day, seeking out men who do evil and hurrying them to an early grave."

I wondered how many of those she'd find at the church. "That was a great story." I beamed at him, my mind already working at how I could include it in my latest novel. I could substitute the evil baron for an evil cattle rancher. Mattie Doon could become the sweet, innocent school teacher of Gulliver's Crossroads. Yes, that could work.

"You said ghosts, plural," Lucas pointed out.

"That I did. It's an old church. Plenty of ghosts roam those grounds." Simon eyed us closely. "Some of them still alive."

Lucas leaned forward. "What do you mean by that?"

Simon took a long pull on his pint. "Well, some ghosts are just memories of things gone wrong, aren't they?"

"Like…" I prodded.

He stared at the ceiling a moment. "'Twere ten years ago now. One morning, the vicar came running into the pub shouting the church had been robbed. Imagine that. Someone robbing God himself?"

"What was missing?" Lucas asked.

"Well, now, you'd have to ask the vicar, but I believe there was some silver and whatnot."

"Did they find out who took it?" I asked.

"Well, the rectory—that's where the vicar lives—was being renovated at the time and everyone assumed it was the workmen. Took advantage. That sort of thing."

"I'm guessing it wasn't the workmen," I said.

He beamed at me as if I'd said something particularly brilliant. "Exactly. For you see, the vicar discovered the curate was missing."

"Isn't a curate like an assistant?" I asked.

Simon nodded. "The police decided he must have gotten tired of his duties and run off with the goods. The family was horrified. Insisted that he would have never done such a thing, but..." Simon shrugged. "Innocent people don't run now, do they?"

I wasn't sure that was true, but I didn't want him to stop telling the story. "Did the police ever find the curate?"

"They did not. No sign of him anywhere." Simon leaned forward sending a waft of stale beer breath my way. "They say that until he atones for his sin, part of the curate's soul will be forever trapped inside the church. A living ghost."

#

"That's the nuttiest thing I ever heard," I told Lucas when we were finally on the road again. The bartender, whose name had turned out to be Terry, had given us a gallon of petrol and very clear directions to the inn. And, while it was still raining, visibility had improved somewhat. Lucas had insisted on driving which was fine with me. Simon had launched into more ghost stories and I'd managed to down three Irish coffees. I wasn't sure if I was going to pass out or be up all night. "Do you suppose it's true?"

We passed a small square of grass edged with daffodils and more Georgian stone cottages covered in purple wisteria. A few doors down from the pub was a Tudor-era white-washed building with an A-frame sign out front declaring it a tea room. At the opposite end of town from the pub loomed the church, its bell tower stabbing at the leaden sky. Out front, grave stones scattered higgledy piggedly across a well-trimmed lawn.

"What's true?" Lucas was focused on the road ahead which seemed more muddy than it should be, as if there'd been a landslide over the road.

"About the curate? About some of the ghosts of Chipping Poggs still being alive."

"Simon is an old man fond of telling tall tales. I wouldn't put too much stock in what he says."

He might have a point, but still. It had been an odd thing to say. I sensed there was a mystery here in Chipping Poggs and my mystery hunting bone was tingling. Hopefully it wouldn't be another murder. I'd had my fill of those back home in Astoria. I had an unfortunate habit of finding bodies in studies, bathtubs, and even a cabana once. I wasn't necessarily going to give up amateur sleuthing, but I wouldn't mind if next time someone else found the body.

We left the village and were now driving through a copse of trees. Their thick branches stretched in an arch over the road, blotting out what little could be seen of the dark sky. As Simon promised, the drive leading to the manor house was clearly marked with massive iron gates standing wide to welcome travelers. From one of them hung a sign that read "Wytham Manor Inn" in fancy curlicue lettering.

The rain had washed out some of the gravel leading to a few jarring potholes. "You'd think someone would fix this road," I complained as the car bellied out on one of the more extreme potholes. "Isn't this place supposed to be posh?"

"I imagine it keeps the riffraff out." Simon sounded amused.

"Holy shibblets," I gasped as the manor house came into view.

Lucas gave an amused snort. "It's quite something, isn't it?"

"You said it."

Lights sparkled from a myriad of oriel windows, throwing the manor into relief against the stormy sky. I could make out the triangle points of several gables and a bristle of chimneys marching along the roof. There must be fireplaces galore.

Gravel crunched beneath our tires as Lucas pulled up to the front door. A set of porchlights glowed warmly, revealing a heavy wooden door.

"This will make a perfect headquarters." Lucas smiled happily. "Absolutely the right spot. I couldn't have chosen better myself."

Frankly, the place was kind of spooky. "Sure. Looks great."

"You go inside," Lucas said. "I'll grab the bags."

With a quick nod, I stepped out into the rain and dashed for the entrance. There was only a slight overhang of stone to prevent a person from getting completely drenched. I wasn't sure if I should ring the doorbell like you would at a house, or just walk in like with a hotel. I decided on the later—this was an inn, after all—and tried the door handle. It was unlocked.

The entry hall was lavish in the extreme. Dark wood paneling lined every wall with floorboards stained to match. To the left was a marble fireplace topped with an ornate gilt framed mirror and just beyond it was a door leading to what I imagined was one wing of the house. Dead center of the entry was a small, antique table on top of an antique Persian rug in reds and blues that looked hand woven. In the middle of it sat a simple cut glass vase filled with pink hot-house roses. Above it hung a glittering crystal chandelier. Understated, but elegant. To the right of the hall was another door and a grandfather clock that appeared nearly as old as the manor itself. Straight ahead a staircase led up to the first floor and next to it was a long, dark hall.

I hesitated, worried about dripping all over the expensive carpets. The place definitely looked like a private home, not a public inn.

Not sure how to proceed, I cleared my throat. "Hello?"

A head poked out of the doorway on the left. It was a round head with a wild tuft of ginger hair on top. Little round glasses perched on the end of a pug nose. "Hullo."

"We're looking for a place to stay the night. This is the inn, right?"

He grinned and the rest of him appeared. He was round as a butter ball and barely taller than I was. I'd put him at close to sixty, though his face was unlined. Bright blue eyes appeared big and buggy behind his glasses. He slipped them off and stuck them in his breast pocket.

"Rupert Beaton, innkeeper. At your service." He extended his hand and gave mine a warm shake.

"Are you one of the Wythams?" I asked, curious.

"Oh, no. They hired me to run the place. Feels like mine, though." He looked around, chest puffed out with pride. "You're American, aren't you?"

"For my sins." I grinned. "Do you have a room available?"

"Sure enough. If you don't mind a ghost or two."

Chapter 3
Is The Truth Insulting?

The door banged open on a gust of wind, and I nearly jumped out of my skin. It was only Lucas carrying our suitcases. He set them down inside the entry and slammed the door shut behind him. He gave us a disarming grin. "All set?"

"Mr. Beaton says there are ghosts," I blurted. "The old man, Simon, down at the pub said the manor wasn't haunted."

"Please. Call me Rupert. Simon is incorrect. We do have ghosts, but they're not *bad* ghosts," Rupert said eagerly. "They're actually quite polite as long as you don't go around mucking in their business. Now, let's get you two settled in." He waddled over and grabbed both our suitcases as if they were feather light. "Follow me."

I expected to be taken to an office or check in desk, but instead he clomped up the stairs with us hot on his heels. "We have several guests staying with as at the moment." His voice echoed in the staircase which was paneled the same as the entry hall. "But not to worry, we have plenty of room. In fact, I've a lovely room just at the end of the hall. It overlooks the gardens. Which, of course, you can't see at the moment what with it being almost dark, but they are stunning."

"The end of the hall" proved to be a very long walk. We passed at least five doors on each side of the hallway.

I wondered if they led to bedrooms, bathrooms, or something else entirely. Finally Rupert stopped in front of a door marked with a brass six. He reached into the pocket of his brown corduroy pants, pulled out one of those large, black iron keys that look like they're from the middle ages, and unlocked room six.

"Here we are," he said cheerfully as he snapped on the light. "The honeymoon suite."

Hoo boy. I'd only fairly recently come to terms with Lucas as my boyfriend. The honeymoon suite seemed like an awful lot of pressure, but I told myself not to be a ninny and followed Rupert into the room and stopped still.

Half the room was taken up by a massive four poster bed mounded high with fluffy pillows and canopied in layers of rich fabrics. The idea of the shenanigans that could happen in a bed like that left me a little flustered. There was also a charming little antique vanity in the bay window, a cozy seating area next to a smaller version of the fireplace downstairs, and the prerequisite crystal chandelier. It was all tastefully done in duck egg blue and varying shades of beige and chocolate.

Rupert set the suitcases on the floor next to a large wardrobe. "The lavatory is through there," he said, pointing to a door that was discretely cracked open. "There is no mini bar in the room, but the hotel bar is open until midnight so feel free to join us. The instructions for the television are in the bedside table."

"Don't you want us to fill something out?" Lucas asked, setting the suitcases down at the end of the bed.

"Once you've settled, stop by my office. That's the door I'm came out," Rupert said directly to me. I nodded to show I understood. "We'll get everything squared away. Have you eaten?"

We assured him we had not. My stomach rumbled as if to put an emphasis on the point. Rupert politely ignored it.

"The kitchen is open until ten. You may eat either in the restaurant or the bar. Most guests find the bar cozier. We also provide room service, though most of our guests prefer to come down. Plus, you'll be there already since you have to sign the register." He beamed happily as if it were all settled. "I'm certain you'll get on just fine with the rest of our guests. And on such a dreadful night, what's better than a tipple and some conversation?"

"What indeed?" Lucas said mildly, his gray eyes sparkling with amusement.

"Thank you very much, Rupert," I said. "Give us a few minutes and we'll be down."

"No rush," Rupert assured us. He pulled the door shut behind him as he exited, leaving us to our own devices.

"This is surprisingly nice," I said, poking around the room. I opened one of the nightstand drawers and found—instead of the expected Gideon Bible—a Stephen King novel. Just what I needed in a haunted mansion. "I was expecting something more...chintzy."

"You watch too many of those old British shows," Lucas said, his voice muffled as he hung his coat in the wardrobe. "Hyacinth Bucket isn't exactly a reliable slice of British life."

I shrugged. "Maybe."

"I have an idea." When Lucas turned around there was a wicked look on his face.

I eyed him askance. "What are you up to?"

"Me?" he asked innocently as he stalked toward me slowly.

"Yes, you." I was suddenly all warm and tingly inside. All thoughts of food vanished. "What's your idea?"

He glanced from me to the bed and back, that wicked smile never leaving his face. Then he pulled me against his chest and kissed me.

# # #

Rupert's office was exactly how I visualized a proper English study to be: leather upholstered furniture, heavy velvet drapes, and hunting scenes on the walls. It was small, but comfortable. More lord-of-the-manor than operating hotel. After filling out the registry and forking over a credit card, Rupert directed us past the staircase and down the dark hall I'd noticed earlier.

The floorboards creaked under our feet and the faces of cranky old men stared back at us gloomily from the walls. I noticed one of the paintings was of an elderly man from approximately the early 1800s. He glared down at me from beneath bushy eyebrows, his sideburns slicing down his cheeks like angry arrows. I squinted at the brass plaque beneath the portrait. It was the 17th Baron Wytham and he was every bit as unfortunate looking as Simon had promised. Creepy. No wonder this place was haunted. It practically asked for it.

The bar was through a door at the end of the hall. It looked much like the pub in town except the bar itself was far more upscale—mahogany, I think—highly polished, and smooth. Instead of small, cottage style windows, the manor's windows were tall and arched, giving what I imagined was a good view of the garden during the day. At the moment they were dark and streaked with rain. The occasional flash of lightening in the distance revealed eerie shadows beyond the panes of glass. I shuddered. It was the perfect night for evil deeds.

A large, marble fireplace was lit, warming the space. Comfortable armchairs in aubergine velvet clustered around dark wood tables that looked to be at least a hundred years old or more. Three guests sat at the bar. The rest of the guests sat in groups at tables. There were ten guests in all, counting Lucas and myself.

A slender black man stood behind the bar. He wore a light blue cashmere sweater with a black apron over it. His name tag read "Bill."

"What will it be, folks?" Bill called cheerfully. A dimple flashed in his left cheek. "Beef bourguignon is the special tonight, and I've a lovely red wine to go with it."

I nodded and Lucas said, "Sounds good. Two, please."

"Coming right up. Make yourselves at home."

We were about to settle ourselves at a table near one of the windows when a solitary guest near the fire waved us over. She looked to be early thirties and was wearing a flowy blue peasant top over jeans along with a string of gemstone beads, also in blue. Her long, reddish brown hair was pulled back from her face in a thin braid revealing a pert, freckled nose and grayish-green eyes. "I'm Jezebel Montgomery. You can call me Jez. You're Americans, aren't you? Where from?" Her own accent marked her as American.

"I'm Viola Roberts," I said. "And this is my boyfriend, Lucas Salvatore. We're from Oregon."

"Oh, I love Oregon. Have a seat." She patted the chair next to her, so I sat down. Lucas sat across from us. "I'm from California. Eureka." Jez beamed at us. "My mom runs a coffee shop bookstore there. Tarot reading and séances on the side. But, there just aren't enough ghosts there for me. Interesting ones, I mean."

"I take it you have an interest in the supernatural?" Lucas asked.

"Well, if by supernatural you mean ghost hunting, then yes. I'm a paranormal investigator. That's why I'm here. So many ghosts." She waved exuberantly at the room, which I took to mean the entire house. "So much material for my website. I write a paranormal travel blog, too."

"You actually believe in them? Ghosts?" I could hardly keep the incredulity out of my voice. I mean, okay, so the whole ghost story thing was fun, but real ghosts? Nope. Didn't believe in them. When I'd nearly been thrown down the stairs of a so-called haunted hotel in Florida, people had latched onto the ghost theory. Naturally, it had turned out to be a cold-blooded but very human killer.

"Well, yes and no. I mean, I think there are things in this world we can't explain with our current knowledge of science, but I'm not sure that ghosts exist as we think of them. But I find the whole thing fascinating, so I made a career of it." She eyeballed me. "I also read palms and tarot sometimes. My mom taught me. I can read for you if you like."

Bill arrived with our wine and our dinner, saving me from responding. We dug in to the meaty, boozy rich stew. It was divine. Jez already had a glass and had assured us she'd eaten.

"How long have you been here?" I asked her. "At the hotel, I mean."

"Got here two days ago. Haven't been able to do a lot of investigating yet, but I've picked up some interesting readings on my equipment." She took a sip of what looked and smelled like cider.

"Interesting, how?" Lucas asked.

"Yesterday I got a temperature spike in the ballroom. It plummeted by twenty degrees. That's not normal."

We both agreed that it wasn't. Although I wasn't prepared to leap to the ghost conclusion.

"My EMF detector—that's Electro Magnetic Field detector—had a nice jump into the paranormal range, too. 6.0. Anything between 2.0 and 7.0 is a good sign." She propped her elbows on the table and her sleeve fell back to reveal a small infinity tattoo on her left wrist. "All in all, it's very encouraging."

"What do you plan to do if you find one?" I asked. "A ghost, I mean. Exorcise it?"

"Not my bag," she said, taking another sip of cider. "Especially here at the manor. Ghosts are part of the charm of the place. Who wants to ruin that?"

"But if someone did?" I pressed, curious.

"I dunno. Wave some sage around." She mulled it over, a frown line forming between her brows. "I should probably figure that out."

"Probably," I said tartly. Jez didn't seem phased by my snarky tone, but Lucas quickly changed the subject.

"I suppose you've had a chance to meet some of our fellow guests." He nodded toward the far corner. "Them for instance."

I glanced over. The couple appeared to be in their forties, though in the dim light of the bar it was hard to tell. They ate silently, barely looking at each other. He wore dark cords and a button down denim shirt. She wore an unflattering mid-calf length dark skirt and a shapeless beige cardigan over a white blouse.

"That's James and Monica Carsely," Jez said, keeping her voice low. "Odd couple. They almost never speak to each other. Very stiff and awkward. I mean, I know the British can be standoffish, but they take it to the next level. I offered to read tarot for her. She seemed interested, but her husband glared at her, so she made some lame excuse. They're suspicious, if you ask me."

I wondered if Monica had really been all that interested, or if Jez had badgered the poor woman and her husband had simply helped her escape. I eyed them carefully. They were odd, for sure, but suspicious?

"Why suspicious?" I asked.

"Everyone here is relaxing, having a good time. But them?" She frowned. "It's like they're waiting for something."

Which was interesting, though not proof of anything. I watched the Carsleys as they finished their dinner and got up from the table. He walked out of the bar without a second glance, shoulders squared, head high. She followed him, head down, shoulders bowed. I frowned. Interesting, indeed.

"What about the people at the bar?" Lucas asked, jarring me from my musing.

"Now there's an interesting bunch," Jez said cheerfully. "The old guy with the trilby hat just arrived today. He's some kind of retired army guy. We haven't been introduced. The couple with him...she's a professor at Oxford and he's her husband. They're here studying architecture or old books or something. Haven't had much of a chance to talk to them yet. They're the Huxton-Barringtons."

"That's unusual," I said. "I'm not sure I've heard of a man with a hyphenated name."

"Oh, it's actually not that unusual in England." She turned slightly in her chair. "The woman at the table behind me is Marilyn Toppenish. She arrived the same day I did."

Marilyn Toppenish was in her sixties, or possibly even early seventies, with a round figure and fluffy fake-blonde hair piled on top her head in a semblance of a beehive. Her face was heavily made up and her frosted pink lipstick matched her blouse. She wore a pair of silver, rhinestone-encrusted cat's eye reading glasses on the end of her nose. She was knitting furiously, fuzzy blue yarn pooled on her lap, but her bright eyes watched the rest of us with keen interest. Marilyn was a busybody. Of that I'd no doubt. She'd be the kind of person who'd spy on her neighbors with binoculars.

"Now, he's interesting." Jez's voice interrupted my thoughts. The man she indicated was fifty-ish and skinny, with haunted eyes and a hard edge to him. His clothes were dated and dingy, out of place in a swanky manor house hotel like this, and his thinning brown hair was in need of a cut. "He arrived this morning shortly after the old army guy. I heard him check in. Gave his name as Jeffrey Blodgett. Don't know anything about him, but he's creepy looking, don't you think?"

I did think. In fact, if I were writing this scene, I would have made Blodgett the murderer.

Chapter 4
Bump in the Night

I jerked awake, disoriented and irritated. Only the faint blue glow from the cable box illuminated the room. Right, the manor house. Beside me, Lucas snored on, blissfully unaware of the howling wind outside. Except it wasn't the wind that had woken me. Was it?

A crash, followed by loud voices echoed up from the entry hall below. *That* was what woke me up. Had to be.

I slid out of bed, grabbed my robe, and wrapped it around me as I padded barefoot to the door. Cracking it open just a hair, I peered out. The hallway—papered in blue and gold stripes— was faintly lit by sconces at intervals along the wall. They must have been the type that could be dimmed because they had clearly been turned to their lowest setting. The voices were more distinct with the door open. I was pretty sure the male voice belonged to Rupert. The female voice...not sure about that one.

I eased out into the hall, pulling the door shut behind me. Fortunately, the old school latches didn't automatically lock like in modern hotels. I had no idea where Lucas had put the old-fashioned skeleton key. I tiptoed toward the top of the stairs, straining to hear what was going on below.

"You've got to do something," the female voice snapped out. Her tone was tight and clipped, the accent posh. London maybe.

Grabbing the stair rail, I crouched down a little, leaning over so I could see the entry. Below stood a woman dressed in a voluminous black pea coat. The fabric was soaked, as was her dark hair. She dripped a puddle around her all while Rupert fussed with a cloth, trying to mop up the mess.

"I'm sorry, miss, but it's a deluge out there. Nothing I can do until morning."

"You can call someone," she snarled. "Get a tow truck out here. I'm in a hurry." She tapped one nude colored heel imperiously.

Bill came into view. His sweater and apron had been swapped out for red flannel pajamas and a robe. "There's only one towing company for miles, and they won't come out here. Not at night. Not in this storm. I'm sorry." Bill's tone was firm. Clearly the woman's haughty attitude didn't faze him.

"I can put you up for the night," Rupert offered. "Dry your clothes for you. We'll call the garage in the morning."

"Fine," she huffed. "As long as it's first thing."

"He won't answer the phone before nine." Bill seemed amused by the woman's frustration.

She growled out something about backwater dumps. I carefully backed away from the stairs, ignoring the sharp stab of disappointment. No ghost. No murder. Just an annoying, entitled woman who'd had car trouble and ended up at the nearest shelter. She was lucky it was a nice place like this and not some horrible, seedy motel.

As I climbed back into bed, Lucas rolled over and wrapped his arm around my waist, snuggling in. I smiled a little to myself. It was nice, cuddling like this. That was my last thought as I drifted off to sleep.

# # #

The next morning the storm had let up. Weak sun streamed around the cracks in the heavy drapes, nudging us out of bed. I could smell bacon, which was all the encouragement I needed.

Skipping makeup, I ran a quick brush through my dark hair and hurried into a pair of jeans, a plain gray t-shirt, and a navy hoodie. I crammed my feet into flip flops, and left Lucas snoring in bed. I figured I could take a shower and do the proper makeup thing later. Right now I needed coffee and a whole lot of that bacon.

The dining room was a cheery surprise. The walls were painted a warm, butter yellow. The large windows had sheer, cream draperies. They were pulled back to reveal a wide flagstone paved patio area and beyond that a garden still dripping with the prior night's rain and rioting with color from early blooming crocuses and daffodils. A stone cupid peered from under a budding lilac. Inside, small tables were scattered neatly about, their linen cloths matching the drapes in color. Each had a bud vase containing a single daffodil. Along one wall was a buffet groaning under the weight of several silver chafing dishes. I headed straight for the coffee urn.

"What a night, huh?" Jez appeared at my side looking bright eyed and bushy tailed. Her hair was up in a bouncy ponytail. "Did you hear the ruckus? Thought we were being burgled."

"Yeah," I admitted. "Woke me up. It was just some woman that had a break down."

"Not a break down," Jez said, giving me a knowing look. "She literally ran her car off the road and into a ditch. You'd think these people would be used to driving in the rain."

"You'd think."

"I'll leave you to it. Plenty to eat. Coffee's mediocre, though."

I filled my cup, dumped in sugar and milk—there was no cream, the British are weird like that—and took a sip. She was right. The coffee was weak and the quality sub-par. Mediocre was putting it kindly. Still, coffee was coffee. I'd never been much of a tea drinker.

Setting my cup at one of the empty tables, I returned to the buffet and loaded up a plate. There was so much to choose from: toasted and buttered crumpets, sausage links, both British and American style bacon, scrambled and fried eggs, baked beans, sautéed mushrooms, toast, and pots of jam and butter. There were also containers of cold cereal, a selection of flavored yogurts, and a large bowl of fresh fruit. I was sure to gain twenty pounds from breakfast alone.

I sat down to eat and pulled out my phone. I'd promised to call my best friend, Cheryl Delaney, when we reached Oxford. Unfortunately the storm had thrown me off. Realizing I'd forgotten, I opened up my instant messaging to find demands to know if I was okay and threats to dispatch the entire Astoria police force if I didn't answer.

Likely she was still asleep, but I quickly sent an answer:

Recall the rescue squad. Everything is okay. Big storm last night and we got lost. Ended up in this cute little village called Chipping Poggs. Locals say the church is haunted! We're staying at the manor house, which is an inn. Very posh! More later.

I was half-way through breakfast when Lucas joined me looking sleepy and tousled. "Bad news," he said, sitting down with only a cup of coffee and a pot of yogurt. How he considered that breakfast, I'll never know.

"I love bad news," I said dryly. "Give it to me."

"Rupert says the storm is over, but we're stuck."

"Stuck?"

"As in, the roads are flooded and we can't get out of town."

I set down my fork. "You're kidding me." And picked up a piece of bacon.

"Unfortunately, not. Chipping Poggs and the manor are both on high ground so we can get around locally, but thanks to the unprecedented rainfall, the surrounding roads have been completely washed out. We can't go anywhere. The entire Cotswolds is flooded."

"How long?"

"If it doesn't rain again, a couple days."

I chewed thoughtfully on another piece of bacon. "Well, it could be worse. There's plenty of food, even if the coffee's not great, and we've got a haunted mansion to explore." There was also the tea room in town. Visions of scones with clotted cream and jam danced in my head.

Lucas grinned, his gray eyes crinkling slightly at the corners. "Glad you're taking this so well."

I shrugged. "How am I supposed to take it? Nothing I can do. No sense getting all worked up about it. Might even start my next novel. I've been thinking about moving into Regency romances."

His smile widened. "Could be an interesting project for you. We're certainly in the right place and aren't they always popular?"

"Very. By the way, you missed the excitement last night." I told him about the late arrival and Jez's input on the situation.

"It was pretty bad out there," he said. "Remember how hard it was for us to see. She's lucky she didn't end up much worse off."

I agreed wholeheartedly. I also wondered where the new arrival was this morning. Bet she wasn't too happy about being told she couldn't leave. She'd seemed in an all-fire rush last night.

"Speak of the devil," I muttered.

The woman from last night appeared in the doorway. She was dressed in neatly pressed black trousers, a red silk blouse, and those nude heels. Her ink black hair was cut in a chin length bob and sleeked within an inch of its life, not a single hair out of place. Her high cheekbones, almond shaped eyes, and naturally golden skin gave away her Asian heritage. She wore the bare minimum of makeup—likely whatever had been in her purse: Eye liner, mascara, nude lipstick, and a light dusting of bronzer. Frankly, she didn't need even that much. She was gorgeous, in a cold sort of way.

She surveyed the room for a moment, her expression giving nothing away. Then she strode toward the buffet, her heels clacking smartly on the parquet floor. She carefully poured a small amount of cereal into a bowl, added milk, and then walked straight toward us.

"You're Lucas Salvatore," she said without preamble, looming over him.

"Yes, I am. Would you like to join us?" If he was surprised at being recognized, he didn't show it.

"Thank you." She glanced around as she took a seat at our table, taking in Jez and the professor and her husband. "The rest of these people seem quite low class." Her gaze skimmed over me as she said it, which set my hackles on end, but I pretended I hadn't noticed her inclusion of me. "Anyway, I have greatly enjoyed your books on my travels."

"Thank you. What do you do?" he asked politely.

"Pharmaceuticals. I travel a great deal and I enjoy reading rather than rotting my brain in front of a screen." She took a dainty bite of her cereal. I hoped she'd slop milk down her front, but she didn't.

"I'm surprise you deign to read fiction," I said snarkily.

Lucas gave me a warning look, but I ignored him. The woman was a world class snob.

"Only well written fiction," she said. "And none of that romance trash."

Even Lucas winced over that one.

"Oh, really?" I said, a dangerous edge to my tone.

"I'm Lavender Wu," the woman said. She turned cool, copper eyes to me. "And who are you?"

I gritted my teeth. Was there a way I could dump salt in her tea without her noticing?

"This is my girlfriend, Viola Roberts," Lucas said.

She gave a moue of distaste. Now I wanted to punch her.

"Did you hear that we're stuck? The roads out of town are flooded." I took a certain satisfaction in the look of frustration that crossed her face. She clearly thought she was too important to be locked in with the yokels. I wondered why. Her clothes were nice, but not *that* nice. And we were staying at a manor house, for crying out loud.

"Most annoying," she said. "I have several important appointments and now I shall have to reschedule them all. What a waste of time. Why couldn't I at least have been marooned somewhere more civilized?"

Neither Lucas nor I bothered to answer as the question was likely rhetorical. Besides, civilized or not, so far the manor house was intriguing, if a little spooky, and

I was looking forward to exploring the village. It had been hard to see it in the rain.

Lucas finished his yogurt and went to get toast and bacon. The minute he left the table, Lavender turned cold eyes on me. "I don't see what someone like Lucas Salvatore is doing with the likes of you." She gave me a look of pure disgust. Whether her expression was because I was a woman of lush curves or because of some other reason, there was no telling. Whatever the case, she obviously felt my boyfriend should be with someone like her. I wondered if I should point out she wasn't his first groupie to try and get rid of me, nor would she be the last.

"I'm pretty sure it's because Lucas prefers brains and character over shallow bullshit," I said lightly. I resisted the urge to scratch her eyes out. Lucas was, after all, with me. I'd no reason to be jealous.

If looks could kill, I'd have been a corpse. She stood abruptly and stormed from the room, leaving her dirty dishes behind.

"What crawled up her backside?" Lucas asked mildly as he sat down with a plate of food and a fresh cup of coffee.

"Apparently she can dish it, but she can't take it."

He sighed heavily. "I'm guessing you insulted her."

"Only if the truth is insulting."

"I assume in this instance it was."

I gave him a sly smile. "Very."

He chewed a forkful of scrambled eggs. "What's the plan for today?"

"It's still kind of mucky out there, so I thought I'd poke around the inn. I bet there's plenty to explore. Want to join me?"

He shook his head. "You go ahead. I need to get a chapter written. Maybe we can check out the village later?"

"Sounds good." I gave him a peck on the cheek and sauntered off to explore. Maybe I'd even find one of those ghosts.

Chapter 5
Ghost Hunting

The dining room was across the hall from the bar where we'd had dinner the previous night. The door stood open, the bar empty. I was betting that due to the results of the downpour, it would be full by noon. Anything to relieve the boredom.

Back down the hall toward the entry were two more doors. The first led into what I would call a family room, but no doubt had a posh name like drawing room or parlor. It was currently empty, but looked like a nice place to congregate. It had cozy couches and chairs, game tables, and a large fireplace already laid with firewood.

As I continued down the hall, Rupert popped out of his office. "How was breakfast?"

"Fantastic, thanks." I didn't mention the sub-par coffee.

"My partner, Bill, recently took over the cooking."

"Well, he's doing a fine job."

Rupert gave me a relieved smile and disappeared back into his office. I continued on my tour.

The second door, the one closest to the front door, led into a library. The walls were covered in bookshelves groaning under the weight of thousands of books. It contained everything from ponderous historical tomes to light hearted paperback romances. The fireplace in this room was smaller, a fire already dancing merrily, throwing a warm glow into the room. A writing desk butted up against one window, its wide surface neatly set with a pad of paper, envelopes, a selection of pens, and a letter opener shaped like a medieval knight's dagger.

I was about to step inside when I realized the room was already occupied. One man, dressed in a forest green sweater, stood next to a shelf, a small, leather bound volume in one hand as he faced a second man. The first man's back was to me so I couldn't tell who it was, but I recognized the second man immediately. It was James Carsley, his face contorted in rage, ears bright red.

"Listen you—"

"No you listen," the first man's voice was slightly muffled. "I am not interested in your opinion…"

James Carsley let out a slew of curse words that would make a longshoreman blush. "You're going to pay for this…"

I carefully backed out of the room and pulled the door shut behind me. I wanted desperately to listen in, but there was no way to do so without getting caught. To say I was disappointed was putting it mildly. Ah, well, there was plenty more to explore. And maybe I could get something out of James later. Although somehow I doubted it. He hadn't seemed the chatty type.

I was about to head upstairs when a loud voice with a heavy Northern accent barked out, "There you are! I've been looking for you."

I turned to find Marilyn Toppenish beaming at me from the bottom of the stairs. She was wearing a polyester twinset in mauve which looked like she'd dug it out of the bargain bin at a thrift shop. Her glasses hung from a silver chain around her neck and strawberry shaped earrings dangled from her lobes. Her makeup was once again caked on, half lost in the heavy creases of her face which ran into her neck and melted the whole thing into an enormous waddle. She clutched a tote bag to her massive bosom. Its turquoise and hot pink flowers badly clashed with her clothing.

I gave her a curious look. "You have?"

"Marilyn Toppenish." She stuck out her hand and I took it reluctantly only to receive a surprisingly firm handshake. "Come along. I was going to set up in the drawing room before the best seats are taken."

So, I was right. There was a fancier name for it. "Sure." I followed her into the dim room where she snapped on a table lamp and ensconced herself in a large, overstuffed chair the color of a cranberry. "You said you were looking for me?" I prompted.

She pulled a skein of forest green yard from her bag. "Right. You're Viola Roberts. The one here with that hunky thriller writer."

"Lucas, yes. He's my boyfriend."

Her eyes lit up with carnal delight. "Lucky you."

I lifted a brow. "Lucky him."

She sputtered with laughter. "You're a bold one."

"Takes one to know one. Now, what can I help you with?"

"I looked you up on the internet." She eyed me over her knitting needles. There was a cleverness there, but maybe too much cleverness.

"And?"

"Seems you like to solve murders. Regular Miss Marple."

I didn't say anything. What was there to say? She wasn't wrong. Except that I wasn't nearly as old as Miss Marple and I'd never worn tweed in my life.

She lifted an eyebrow. "I know a thing or two about murder." Since she so clearly wanted me to ask, I did. "Do you? What do you know?"

"That would be telling, now, wouldn't it? But I know about a murder 'as happened right 'ere in this village. And I know who done it." Her needles clacked together and her eyes glinted. She was a woman who liked knowing things other people didn't. And she liked lording over them with it. I gave a sound of disgust and stood.

"Listen, Marilyn, I've got no time for games. You want to talk, you know where I am." I stalked out of the room. Behind me I could hear Marilyn tutting. I was pretty sure the only thing offended was her pride. I was familiar with her type. She wanted to manipulate me, but I had better things to do than put up with her nonsense. Murder in this village, my backside. The place looked like it had never seen so much as a traffic accident.

"Oh, Viola, there you are. You want to help me ghost hunt?" It was Jez. She had donned a pair of black rimmed glasses which made her look adorably nerdy.

"I thought you hunted ghosts at night."

"Well, night is best," she admitted. "But ghosts don't go away just because it's daylight. At least, that's the prevailing theory."

"Sure. Makes sense." It totally didn't. I couldn't believe this woman believed in ghosts. I mean, she came off as totally sane and everything.

"So? You up for it?"

"What do we have to do?"

She whipped out a small, black device. "I'll carry this EMF detector. It'll alert us to the energy of nearby ghosts. You can carry this." She handed me a digital camera. "Video the investigation. Just in case."

"In case of what?"

"We run into any ghosts, of course. We want to get them on tape."

I stared at the little silver camera. "Right."

"We'll start in the attic."

"You sure Rupert wants us poking around up there?" I asked, hoping that Rupert was dead set against it. On the one hand, ghost hunting would keep me busy. On the other, poking through dusty attics wasn't exactly my idea of a good time.

"He's thrilled. He and Bill have given me the run of the place." She started up the stairs with me trailing reluctantly behind her. "I think he's hoping I find something so he has an official sighting on the record. It would really boost the tourist trade."

I had no doubt. Once we'd reached the second floor—or what the British referred to as the first floor—she led me down the hall past a maid with a cleaning cart. "Morning, Anka," she said cheerfully.

Anka glowered at her, face twisted sourly. She looked to be about my age or a bit older. Her clothes were frumpy and ill-fitting and her graying hair was twisted up in a knot atop her head. She mumbled something in what was clearly not English.

At the end of the hall was a narrow staircase leading up. "These used to be the servants' quarters," Jez explained. "But now they're mostly storage." The floorboard of the landing squeaked ominously beneath her sneaker shod feet. I was wearing flip flops both for comfort and for packing ease. I could feel the chill of the floor beneath the thin soles. Clearly nobody had bothered heating the place. I shivered a little.

The attic was one long hallway with rooms on both sides, and a set of stairs on either end. I poked my head into one of the rooms. It was so small I couldn't imagine it had ever held anything other than a single bed and maybe a bedside table. There wasn't even room for a wardrobe. And the tiny windows were just enough for a little ventilation. The entire place was plunged in eternal gloom. Currently the room had stacks of boxes and crates with just enough room between them to squeeze through.

"Wow, this hotel sure has a lot of crap," I mused.

"I doubt it all belongs to the hotel," Jez said. "The family still owns the place, you know. The Baron Wytham or whatever. Used to be stinking, filthy rich, but over the years they lost most of their money. According to Rupert, they could only afford to keep the place if it earned income. Hence the hotel."

"Clever. As long as they don't need to live here."

"Apparently not. There's a townhouse in London and a villa in Spain. Or was it Portugal? Somewhere like that. I think the villa is a hotel, too."

"That would be an interesting place to stay." I wondered if I could talk Lucas into a trip somewhere sunny. A week in a villa sounded nice and relaxing.

Jez proceeded to walk the hall, waving her EMF reader around. "This is disappointing," she said. "I'm not getting anything."

"Too bad. Listen, I've got to use the toilet. Here." I thrust the camera at her and turned back the way we'd come.

"You're coming back, right?"

But I was already on the staircase and pretended I hadn't heard her. I guess I wasn't cut out for ghost hunting.

# # #

I hadn't been lying. I did need a bathroom. So, I stopped off at the room to use our en-suite. The bedroom was empty, though the curtains had been drawn back and the bed made. Clearly housekeeping had been by, but Lucas was either still in the breakfast room, or had found a quiet place to work.

Taking advantage of the peace and quiet, I took a quick shower and then spent some time on my makeup and hair. Feeling refreshed and invigorated, I figured I'd check in on Lucas. Maybe I could convince him to take a break and visit the village with me.

The breakfast room was empty. The only things left were several mugs, an insulated carafe of hot water, milk, sugar, tea bags, and a jar of instant coffee. The British seemed overly fond of instant coffee, but I was feeling under caffeinated, so I made myself a cup of the stuff.

The drawing room was hopping. Marilyn was still where I'd left her, knitting away. I noticed there was a box of champagne truffle chocolates at her side. Half of them gone. Monica sat at a gaming table near the large bay window with the professor and her husband playing a game of cards. Someone had turned on the radio and the grating sounds of easy listening filled the room. I winced and backed out before anyone saw me and roped me into a boring card game or something.

I doubted Lucas was in the kitchen or Rupert's office and the door to the bar was shut and locked. Maybe he was in the library.

I strolled down the hall, sipping my coffee—surprisingly, not bad—and studying the portraits and landscapes that crammed every inch of wall space. There were a lot of them. The landscapes were pleasant renderings of the countryside around the manor. The portraits were, naturally, of the family's ancestors, including the unfortunate looking baron. I'd half-expected gothic renderings of ghostly images. I was disappointed to find nothing of the sort.

The door to the library was open a crack. Likely that was where Lucas was hiding. I pushed the door open and stepped inside. Someone had drawn the drapes, leaving the room dim and shadowy. The fire still flickered in the fireplace, though it was in need of stoking and the flames had fallen low. A figure was hunched over the desk. Maybe Lucas had come here to work and had fallen asleep. We had stayed up a bit late enjoying that bed. Silly man.

With a sly grin I crept across the room and poked him in the side. "Boo!"

The figure didn't move. And then I saw something silver sticking out of his back. A dagger! My mug hit the carpeted floor with a thud, spraying coffee everywhere, but I didn't notice. "Lucas," I whispered. "Oh, God."

I reached to touch him and the body slumped sideways. The light caught his features and relief flooded me. It wasn't Lucas. It was Jeffrey Blodgett and he was stone cold dead.

Shéa MacLeod

Chapter 6
The Colonel Takes Charge

"What do you mean, the police can't come?" I snapped. Finding the body hadn't exactly had a calming effect on me. You'd think I'd be used to it by now, but no, it still rattled me. I kept seeing the dagger shaped letter opener shoved into Blodgett's back, his dead eyes staring at nothing. And Rupert's calm announcement that the police weren't coming had pushed me over the edge.

He fidgeted, pulling at a loose bit of yarn on his sweater vest. The mustard color clashed with his ruddy complexion. "Well, there used to be a local constable back in the day, but budget cuts, you know. The nearest station is in Chipping Camden and they are, alas, stuck on the other side of the flooded roads, just as we are."

"Then what are we supposed to do?" Lucas demanded. "Surely they don't expect us to just leave the body sitting in the middle of the library. This is a murder scene."

"Er, no. Of course not. That's where Colonel Frampton comes in." Rupert waved over a man who'd been hovering in the shadows. He was tall and thin with a shock of unruly white hair, enough wrinkles to create a road map, and a pair of surprisingly shrewd blue eyes. "The colonel is retired army."

"I also served for a short time with the constabulary up in Yorkshire," the colonel said in a plummy baritone.

His accent was less London and more Northern, like Marilyn's. "I have training in the collection of evidence and the preserving of a crime scene. The police have asked me to take over and preserve the body and crime scene as best I can."

Jez peered at him from her perch on the stairs. "And how do you propose to do that?"

"First I will examine the body and take careful photographs of its position. Then I will wrap it in a clean sheet and store it in the hotel's walk-in fridge."

"With the food?" Marilyn Toppenish looked horrified. Her ample bosom heaved beneath mauve polyester.

"We have two of them," Rupert explained calmly. "I'll have Bill shift all the food into one of them and leave the other for the—er—body."

"Precisely," Colonel Frampton agreed. "We shall also seal off the library until such a time as the proper police arrive."

"There goes any attempt at intelligent pursuits," muttered the professor, her expression turning sour. Her husband gave her an irritated nudge. "What? It's true."

"What I need is someone to assist me," Colonel Frampton continued as if he'd never been interrupted. "Is there anyone here with any sort of police experience?"

"I was with the Israeli Army," Lucas offered. "I can certainly assist in moving the body."

"I've helped the police solve several murders," I said. Everyone turned to stare at me. "Hey, don't look at me. I didn't kill them. I just have a penchant for finding dead bodies." I realized as I said it how bad that sounded. Oh, well. In for a penny, in for a pound, as they say.

Colonel Frampton eyed me with what looked like concern. I gritted my teeth. I was used to those looks from the police back home. I did not need it from a complete stranger. Frampton cleared his throat. "Very well. Mr. Salvatore, if you will assist me, I'm sure we can have everything under wraps in no time at all. Once we've removed the body, Rupert can lock the library door until the police arrive."

Everyone stood around and watched as Lucas carefully used his cell phone to document the body's position. As the flash on his phone went off I realized that Blodgett was wearing a forest green sweater. He'd been the one arguing with Carsley. Interesting.

I took a step back, moving closer to Jez. "You know," I kept my voice low so the others wouldn't overhear. "Somebody should search Blodgett's room."

She stared at me with wide eyes. "Won't the police get pissed off?"

I grinned. "Not if they don't know. We'll be careful. Put everything back where we find it. And we should wear gloves."

She looked eager. "Where will we find gloves?"

"I'm betting housekeeping has plenty. They don't clean those toilets bare handed, believe me." In my early twenties I'd done a stint as a house cleaner. I wore gloves for everything. People are gross.

"There's a supply closet upstairs," she said. "We can check in there. They don't keep it locked. I know because

I needed toilet paper, so I just went and got some. And some extra towels. They never give you enough."

"Okay, let's go."

We slipped up the stairs as quietly as possible. We needn't have bothered. Nobody noticed. They were all too busy fixating on the body removal. Like I said, people are gross.

The supply closet was at the top of the stairs. Jez opened the door and popped inside. "Found 'em." She handed me a pair of pink, rubber gloves. They were thick and a little too big, but they would definitely keep us from leaving fingerprints all over Blodgett's room.

"Do you happen to know which room is his?" I asked.

"Sure. He's in the one next to mine. I don't know how we're going to get in, though."

I held up my key. "These old locks aren't as secure as you might think. The key may not fit, but a little finagling and you can make it work."

She looked doubtful. "If you say so."

Sure enough, a little wiggling around in the lock and the door opened. The drapes were drawn so the room was almost black. We stepped inside and closed the door. I pulled on my pink gloves and flipped on the light switch. The room was similar to the one Lucas and I were staying in, except smaller and lacking a fireplace and seating area. There was a small desk up under the one window and an antique wardrobe next to it. The bed was a sleigh bed instead of a four poster and the color scheme was sage green and a sort of mushroom brown. The tiny bathroom contained a shower and no bathtub.

"I'll search the desk. You look in the wardrobe."

"What are we looking for?" Jez asked.

"Any clue as to what he's doing here or why he was murdered. Somebody at this hotel must have killed him."

"But no one knew him," she said. "Not until he arrived, anyway. He wasn't a pleasant man, but I can't see anyone here killing him."

I gave her a look. "Sure, that's what they say, but I saw him arguing with James Carsley right before I went ghost hunting with you."

"Doesn't mean they knew each other."

"True," I admitted. "But you don't usually go around stabbing people you don't know. I mean unless you're a mugger or something."

The wardrobe doors creaked as Jez opened them. I turned my attention to the desk. The top held a pad of paper with the hotel's logo on it along with matching pens in a ceramic holder painted with apple blossoms. The drawer contained extra pens and paper. Nothing else. I held the notebook up to the light, but it was blank. Didn't look like Blodgett had used it.

"I found something." Jez's voice was tinged with excitement.

That got my attention. "What?"

"His computer." She held up a slim, silver laptop.

"Let me see. Maybe there's a clue in it." She handed it over and I quickly powered it up. "Curses. It's password protected."

"Oh, I've read about this. Try 'god.'"

I gave her a look. "God?"

"Yes. Apparently, it's one of the most used passwords."

Figured. I typed in the letters and got the flashing notice of doom. "Didn't work. How about 'password?'"

"Oh, good one!"

That didn't work either. "Any other thoughts?"

She tapped her chin, gaze lifted to the ceiling as if for inspiration. "123456."

"Seriously?"

"Yep. Try it."

I did. Still nothing. Irked, I stabbed the "1" key several times and hit "enter." To my surprise, it worked. "Look. He's got several files on his desktop. This one's marked 'story.' Wonder what that's about?" I opened it. Inside were several documents marked with chapter numbers. "Looks like Jeffrey Blodgett was working on a novel."

"I wonder if he was any good," Jez mused. "Read it."

I selected a chapter at random and began reading aloud. The story revolved around a character named "Geoffrey Padgett" who was locked up in prison for a 'minor' crime of which he was 'mostly' innocent. The chapter involved a confrontation between some prisoners. "Jeffrey and Juan straightened them out. There would be no more jumping the queue at breakfast. Not with their digits missing."

"Ew. He chopped off their fingers? Because they cut in line? What a nut job."

"Clearly some wacky prison revenge fantasy," I agreed. "Probably trying to get back at people who beat him up." I shook my head and kept reading. "Jeffrey and Juan decided to celebrate their victory over the gang. They went back to their cell. Juan's hands drifted to his jeans button… Oh, my." I slammed the laptop shut, my cheeks turning pink.

"What? What is it?"

"Apparently Jeffrey Blodgett was into more than just revenge fantasy."

Jezz's brow furrowed. "I don't get it…oh!" Her eyes widened. "He was writing prison porn?" She hissed.

"Yep. And I think it was based on reality."

"What do you mean?" she asked.

"Geoffrey Padgett? Come on. If that isn't about as close to Jeffrey Blodgett as you can get, I don't know what is."

"Could be just a fantasy," Jezz pointed out. "Not something that really happened."

"True," I admitted. "But I have a feeling there's more to it. I need to do some research." I handed her the laptop. "Put this back where you found it and let's get out of here."

# # #

We were able to escape Blodgett's hotel room and return the rubber gloves with none the wiser. Then we headed to Jez's room to use her computer.

"You're frowning," she said as she ushered me into the room. Hers was identical to Blodgett's except the drapes were drawn allowing the weak sunshine to illuminate the place. Her soft furnishings were cream and butter yellow and someone had left a vase of fresh yellow roses on her desk.

"There wasn't any blood at the crime scene," I said.

"You're thinking the body was moved?"

I gave her a surprised look.

"What? I watch the Investigation Discovery Channel."

I laughed. "Okay, you got me. Yeah, I'm thinking he may have been killed elsewhere and dragged into the library. It would explain the lack of blood. Still..." I shook my head. "It doesn't make sense. The killer would have had to drag him right through the front hall. Anyone could have seen it. I mean, he wasn't a small man. I'm not sure one person could have moved him. Look at Lucas and the colonel. It took both of them to lift him."

"Yeah. It doesn't make a lot of sense," she agreed. "But what other explanation is there?"

"Who knows? First let's figure out who this guy is."

She sat down at the desk and flipped open her laptop. With a few key strokes she brought up a search on Jeffrey Blodgett. "There's a whole lot of Jeffrey Blodgetts. This one's a doctor."

I squinted at the tiny photo. "Definitely not him. Besides, this one's in New Hampshire."

"I'm getting pages and pages of Blodgetts in the US. Let me add 'UK' to the search." She tapped a couple of keys. "Still tons of the wrong ones. Wait...look at this." She clicked on a link and up came a news article on a trial from nine years ago. "Holy cow," she said. "Would you look at that?"

I squinted at the article. "According to this, he was arrested for possession of stolen property. Eventually they convicted him of burglary as well. I was right about that story! He's been in prison for the last nine years. Only got out a week ago." The article contained a picture of Blodgett from ten years ago along with an image of the officer who'd arrested him.

"And he came here," Jez said. "I wonder why?"

I continued reading. "He stole from a church?"

"Yep. St. Oswin's. It's right here in the village."

I glanced at her. "The haunted church?"

"That's the one. We should go talk to Father Thomas. He can tell us more, I'm sure. He's been here for fifteen years."

"Catholic priest?"

"Nope. Church of England. Technically, I guess he's a reverend, but around here they still call them Father. I like it. It's old fashioned."

"Then I think it's time you and I go to church."

She grinned. "Sounds like a plan."

We found Lucas standing in the entry hall with Colonel Frampton supervising as Rupert locked up the library. Pity. It had been such a cozy, relaxing room. Now the only place to chill was the drawing room with all the other crazies. The colonel pocketed the key. "I'll keep this safe. Chain of custody and all."

"Hey, Lucas," I said, "we're going into the village to explore the haunted church."

"Oh no, dear girl, you are not," Colonel Frampton snapped as if I were one of his troops.

"Excuse me?"

"I need alibis for the time of death. Come along. I've got everyone in the drawing room."

With an eye roll, I followed him into the drawing room, Lucas and Jez hot on my heels. Of course, I knew alibis needed established and I'd hoped to be in on the questioning. I just didn't like that Frampton had got to it before me.

Jez sat down near Marilyn Toppenish who was knitting away as if nothing unusual was going on, a new box of chocolates on the table next to her. Lucas leaned against the mantle looking swoony and brooding. The professor and her husband were sitting at the gaming table and the Carsleys huddled on the couch. Lavender Wu was in the armchair on the other side of Marilyn. She kept throwing Lucas smoldering glances for which I wanted to punch her. I joined the group at the gaming table. Rupert hovered in the background looking ashen and ruffled. Next to him was Bill, calm and collected as ever in a plum colored cashmere sweater. Anka was armed with a feather duster and her usual sullen expression.

Colonel Frampton whipped a pen and notebook out of his breast pocket and cleared his throat. "Now then," he said, his thick, white mustache bobbing up and down like a caterpillar. "As you all know, Jeffrey Blodgett has been killed and the police have put me temporarily in charge. I need to know where everyone was at the time of the murder."

"What time was the murder?" Marilyn asked, popping a chocolate into her mouth.

"I saw Blodgett arguing with James Carsley just after breakfast," I piped up. "Then I found him dead two hours later. That would put the death between nine and eleven this morning."

"Yes, thank you, Ms. Roberts. Very precise." The colonel straightened his navy sports jacket and turned a beady eye on James. "I suppose I should start with you, Mr. Carsley. What were the two of you arguing about?"

"Nothing," James snarled, his face turning a mottled red. He looked out of place in the elegant room with his track suit and scuffed sneakers. His sandy hair was a bit too long and hung in his eyes giving the impression he was hiding. "It was stupid. He'd said something offensive to my wife and I wanted to let him know it wasn't appreciated. He was alive when I left the library."

Monica Carsley kept her gaze on her hands, twisting the hem of her ugly mustard sweatshirt. She never once looked up while James talked. There was no doubt in my mind that he was lying about the argument.

"What time was that?" Colonel Frampton asked.

"Not sure." Carsley shrugged. "Maybe a quarter past nine."

"Where did you go after that?"

"To my room. I needed a shower. I didn't come back down until after Ms. Roberts found the body." James crossed his arms and set his jaw, clearly unwilling to elaborate.

"Anyone who can collaborate?" the colonel asked.

"No," James bit out. He slid a look toward Anka. "Well, she saw me go in the room, but she was gone when I came out."

"Anka?" The colonel turned toward the maid.

"Yes," she said in a thick accent, her tone as sullen as her face. "I woss dere. He vent in room ven he say he did."

"And where were you between nine and eleven?" the colonel asked.

She sighed heavily and rolled her eyes. It reminded me of an exasperated teenager. "Cleaning. Like I supposed to."

"Anyone see you?"

"I was in the kitchen getting ready for lunch the entire time," Bill offered. "Anka came in shortly after ten to help me."

"I saw her earlier," Rupert said. "I took up a load of clean towels. That was just before ten."

"I saw her, too." The professor spoke up. She was a tall, spare woman overly fond of tweeds. "Professor Abigail Huxton-Bennington. I exited my room at nine-twenty and saw the maid cleaning." Which meant that at least from nine to ten, Anka was pretty safe. "I passed her as I went downstairs to the library. I was interested in one of the volumes, so took the opportunity to do a bit of research. I arrived approximately twenty-two minutes past nine and left at ten thirty. It was empty the entire time, save myself. From ten thirty until Ms. Roberts found the body, I was taking tea in the bar."

"True," Colonel Frampton said. "I saw her." I shot him a look. His cheeks turned a bit red. "I saw her enter the library and popped my head in to say hello. Then I went to the bar for, ahem, my own tea. I was there until she came in."

Which was only sort of an alibi. "If it's true that Blodgett wasn't in the library that whole time, he must have left and come back later when he was killed. Where was he?" I asked.

No one seemed to know. There was a lot of shrugging and head shaking.

The colonel cleared his throat again. "Back to the matter at hand. Mrs. Carsley, where were you."

"In here," she said, her voice so soft I almost couldn't hear it. "I was reading a novel."

"It's true," Marilyn Toppenish boomed. "I was here knitting. Your handsome boyfriend was in here, too." Marilyn winked at me. "Working away on that laptop of his."

"I was in bed," Lavender Wu said with an air of disdain. "After last night, I felt I needed a lie down."

"Any witnesses?"

She gave the colonel a dirty look. "Hardly."

"I was ghost hunting," Jez said. "Viola was with me. We never saw Blodgett."

"And I was taking a stroll in the garden," Martin Huxton-Bennington piped up. "I felt the need of fresh air."

"I saw him," Rupert said. "I was working in my office. He passed by the window a couple times."

"Were any of you acquainted with Mr. Blodgett before his arrival at this hotel?" Colonel Frampton asked. Everyone shook their heads in the negative. "Very well. Thank you all. I shall pass this on to the police when they arrive." The colonel put away his notebook and marched from the room. There was quiet for a moment and then everyone started chattering.

There were a whole lot of people with poor alibis. Someone was lying. Certainly James Carsley was, at least about the argument. I needed to know more about Jeffrey Blodgett. I needed to know who had a motive to kill.

Chapter 7
The Case of the Missing Curate

"Now that's over, we're off to the church. Want to come?" I waggled my eyebrows meaningfully. Lucas gave me a baffled look.

"We just found a dead body, Viola. I don't think running around ghost hunting is appropriate."

"Excuse me." I crossed my arms and shot him a glare. Sometimes he could be a real stick in the mud. "*I'm* the one that found the body, not you. And what else are we supposed to do? Sit around feeling gloomy? I for one would like to take my mind off things."

"Dwelling on it won't help anyone," Jez agreed, zipping up her lime green jacket. "Although if we stay here, I could read everyone's Tarot."

"The church it is," Lucas said. "I'll get the car keys."

"Got them right here." I dangled the keys in front of his face.

He gave me a fake smile. He clearly knew I was up to something. "Let's go then."

The three of us clambered into the car. As we took off toward Chipping Poggs, Lucas said, "All right, what's going on?"

I quickly told him about our search of Blodgett's room and Jez finding the prison release papers. Lucas was fit to be tied. "I can't believe you broke into a crime scene."

"We left everything as it was," I assured him.

"And we wore gloves," Jez pipped up. "So we didn't leave fingerprints."

"That makes it so much better," he muttered, shooting me a look of disapproval.

I ignored him. "The article we found online didn't say much about the theft, but it has to have something to do with his death, don't you think? Anyway, we figured we should ask the preacher. He should know more. Plus it's an excuse to get out of that hotel. Those people are weird."

Jez snickered. Lucas gave me a sidelong look, but wisely said nothing, instead focusing on the road ahead which was still muddy and half covered in large puddles.

Since it was daylight and had mostly stopped raining, I was finally able to get a good look at Chipping Poggs. It was exactly as an English village should be: wisteria covered Georgian cottages with the odd Tudor building thrown in for good measure, narrow lanes edged with low-walled gardens, and signposts that pointed vaguely in random directions as if school children had pulled a prank and twisted them around a bit.

A person in a yellow rain slicker and green rubber boots strode along the side of the road. I was pretty sure it was the same woman who'd given us directions yesterday. I waved, but she didn't look up.

The church was built of old stone and half covered in lush, green vines. It looked like at least part of it was medieval, but had likely been revamped sometime in the Victorian era. As was typical of old village churches, it was surrounded by a small graveyard, the headstones poking willy nilly through the grass, leaning as if a gust of wind might blow them over. A giant weeping willow took up half the front yard, softening the place and giving it a dreamy quality. The grounds were surrounded by a low stone wall also covered in vines. To one side of the church, beyond the wall, was a small, matching rectory meant to house the pastor.

Lucas parked in front of the church and the three of us walked up the narrow path between the gravestones. It was wonderfully creepy and oddly soothing. The church door stood open a crack and we stepped into the chill, musty dimness of the old building. Our footsteps echoed loudly on the stone floor. There was no one inside.

Jez glanced around in wonder. "I totally believe this place is haunted. I really need to set up here one night. I bet the readings will be off the charts."

Lucas grimaced, but didn't say anything about ghosts. Instead he said, "Wonder where everyone is?"

"They probably leave it open so people can pray or whatever," Jez said. "Despite the theft ten years ago, this place isn't exactly a hotbed of crime."

I agreed. "We should try the rectory. He's probably having elevenses." What the British called "elevenses" had been a delightful find, as far as I was concerned. It was basically a morning coffee break—or tea break, if you were into that—but with a snack, as well.

"I'll stay here," Jez said, pulling one of her gadgets out of her coat pocket. "I want to get a better feel for the place. I might even catch something on EMP."

Once outside I noticed there was a small, wrought iron gate in the wall near the rectory. We made our way through the damp grass and let ourselves in at the gate, which creaked and groaned as if it didn't want to be bothered. The rectory door opened before we could even knock. A small man stood, neatly dressed in black except for a white dog collar. His wispy white hair only partially covered a pink scalp and little round spectacles made his watery hazel eyes appear big and buggy.

"Visitors! What a pleasant surprise." His broad smile bunched up his pink cheeks and revealed a small dimple next to his mouth. "I'm Thomas Melton. The vicar of St. Oswin the Good. What brings you to my church?"

From inside came the noise of hammers followed by a loud crash. The vicar winced. "Ignore that. I'm having some work done in my study. Roof leaks. Had to get a couple local boys in."

Lucas introduced us, leaving out the part about us being writers.

"We wanted to know more about Jeffrey Blodgett," I blurted.

Father Thomas's forehead wrinkled into a frown and then smoothed out. "Ah! The theft. That was some time ago, but I think I can help. Come in. Come in. I've got the kettle on."

Yep. I'd been right about elevenses.

We followed him into a small eat-in kitchen. The wallpaper was a faded green with large, pink and red roses which clashed with the orange and gold striped curtain. A sink, stove, and fridge of dubious vintage were along one wall with just enough counter space between to slice a loaf of bread. A narrow table was shoved up against the other wall with a chair at each end.

"Take a seat. I'll be right back." There was a great deal of crashing and thumping before Father Thomas returned grasping a metal folding chair. His skin was pinker and shinier than before and he appeared winded, but triumphant. He placed the chair at the empty side of the table and then turned off the electric kettle, which had begun shrieking. As he poured hot water into a tea pot he began to chatter amiably.

"Let me see... It was a good ten years ago now. I'd been vicar here for, oh, five years or so. The former vicar had died, you see. Quite an old man. Eighty-something, I believe. In any case, the rectory was rather worn down at that point, as you can imagine. I don't think it had been touched since the seventies. The *eighteen* seventies." He chortled as he placed a steaming teapot in the middle of the table and turned to collect tea cups from a cupboard above the sink. "Not really, but it was in definite need of some tender loving care. I had been trying to convince the powers that be that it was in dire need of some upgrades when, would you believe, there was a terrible storm. The roof leaked and there was water damage all over the walls and floors in the sitting room and the study. Terrible. Fortunately, it meant that the diocese had to stop dragging their feet and fix the place. Silver lining."

"How lucky," I said dryly.

"Yes. Wasn't it? Although they clearly didn't do a very good job." He set milk and sugar on the table along with a plate of chocolate bourbons. "I hope everyone likes biscuits." I knew he meant cookies. We both assured him we did. "Now, where was I?" He sank into the folding chair which let out a hideous squeak of metal on metal. I was sure he was going to wind up on the floor, but the chair held.

"You got the rectory fixed," Lucas prodded.

"Ah, yes. They'd finished the roof and were just starting on the interior." He poured tea into our cups and waved at the sugar bowl. I helped myself to a large spoonful. "One morning I went over to the church and discovered the door standing wide open. I swear I locked it, but the police said there was no sign of tampering. In any case, some valuable items were missing."

"What sort of items?" Lucas asked.

"An antique silver communion set, for one. Also, there were a couple of very old Bibles worth a few hundred quid each." I knew quid meant pound, which was a bit more than an American dollar with the current exchange rate. "And there were some candlesticks which we used for special occasions."

"Was it the workmen?" I asked. I knew what Simon—the storyteller down at the pub—had claimed, but I wanted the vicar's take.

The vicar beamed at me as if I'd said something particularly brilliant. "That's what everyone thought at first. But then I discovered my curate was missing. He'd only recently arrived. Quite a young man. He seemed so stable though. Such a lovely boy. He was obsessed with old buildings and secret passages. He was acquainted with the family up at the manor house and often spent time there." He frowned as if lost in thought. "In any case, the police decided he must have gotten tired of his duties and run off with the goods. The family was horrified. Insisted that he would have never done such a thing, but…" the vicar shrugged.

"Where does Jeffrey Blodgett fit in?" I asked.

"He was one of the men working on the interior repairs here at the rectory. Initially, he was cleared because everyone believed the curate did it and there was no evidence to prove otherwise. But, you see, about a year after the theft, Jeffrey Blodgett was caught trying to pawn some pieces from the communion service. He was convicted of the theft and sentenced to prison. The police tried to get him to reveal the whereabouts of the missing curate, but he refused. Instead he served his time and eventually was released early on good behavior."

"We heard something of this story down at the pub," Lucas said.

The vicar sighed. "Simon does like to tell the tale. Well, he is right in that the curate was never found. He didn't use his passport and he didn't sell any of the other stolen items. The police assume that Blodgett and the curate were in on it together, but that Robbie—that's the curate—used fake documents and escaped the country leaving Blodgett to get caught. I got a call about a month ago letting me know that Blodgett had been released from prison."

"But why would he come here?" I asked. "Surely he'd want to stay away from the place he'd robbed."

The vicar shrugged. "Who knows the inner workings of a man's soul? Perhaps he felt guilty and wanted to make amends."

Lucas and I exchanged glances. Based on what we'd seen of Blodgett, he wasn't the guilt-ridden type.

I had a sudden inspiration. "Maybe he hid the rest of the loot somewhere here in the village and that's why the police never found it. He could have come back to get it."

"That could very well be," the vicar admitted. "It's certainly a possibility."

There was another loud crash. A freckled face topped by a wild thatch of ginger hair popped around the corner. "Ah, vicar, could you come in 'ere a moment?"

The vicar set down his tea. "If you'll excuse me?"

"Sure," Lucas said.

Curiosity may have killed the cat, but I found it as tempting as catnip. I got up from the table, ignoring Lucas's scowl at my interference, and slipped after the vicar and the repair man. I wanted to see a rectory study for myself. And I wondered what it was that was so urgent that vicar had to be pulled away from his guests.

"Oh, dear," the vicar murmured, stopping dead in the doorway to his study.

"Right?" muttered the repair man.

A second man stood in the room, scratching his head. "It ain't right."

"What is it?" I asked trying to peer around his shoulder.

He attempted to push me back. "A young lady shouldn't be seeing such a terrible thing."

"Nonsense." I was hardly a "young" lady anymore, having passed my fortieth birthday some time ago. I shoved past him into the study and stopped dead. A wet stain spread across the ceiling and down one wall. Where it had soaked into the wall, the sheetrock had crumbled. The workmen had clearly been in the process of cutting that section of the sheetrock out to replace it. Beyond that wall were the desiccated remains of a human body. Around its neck hung a stained dog collar.

"Crikey heck," I muttered. "It's the missing curate."

Shéa MacLeod

Chapter 8
No Such Thing As Coincidence

"Yes, definitely dead." Lucas's voice was a low rumble as he spoke to the police on his cell phone. "We suspect it's the curate who went missing ten years ago, though you'll want to confirm with forensics.... Yes, dead for several years, I expect… I can send some pictures.... Uh, huh...."

"Here, how about a nice cup of tea, Father Thomas," I said, forcing my voice to sound cheerful. The vision of the curate's dead body kept dancing in my head. Somebody had obviously killed him and stuck him behind that wall. Probably the very night he went missing. I remembered old Simon's story and wondered if the theft and murder had something to do with the "ghost" Mrs. Tillicum claimed to see ten years ago.

The workmen had left in a hurry, headed across the green to the pub. Not that I could blame them. I wouldn't mind a stiff drink myself.

"He didn't steal anything, did he?" The vicar's voice was plaintive as I set a cup of hot tea in front of him. I'd added plenty of sugar and a splash of whisky I'd found at the back of the cupboard.

"No, I don't think he did."

"Poor Robbie."

I sat down across from him and patted his hand. "Tell me about Robbie."

The vicar sighed. "That's what we called him. Robbie. But, of course, his name was Robin."

Of course it was. Only the British would call a boy Robin instead of a perfectly respectable Robert. "I'm guessing Robbie caught Blodgett stealing from the church. Blodgett killed him and then walled him up in your study. Since it was under construction, nobody was the wiser." I frowned. "But how did you stand the smell?"

He blanched. "Smell?"

"Yeah. It would have stunk something awful."

"I don't smell too well, I'm afraid. Hyposmia, the doctors call it. Had quite a few sinus infections as a child, plus old age, you know. I wouldn't have smelled a thing." He took a sip of the tea and sighed a little. "It would explain why Mathilde quit, though."

"Mathilde?"

"She was the cleaner for both the church and the rectory. French. Annoying woman. She quit about two months after the theft. Claimed she couldn't stand the state of the place. She thought I was hording food or some such. Frankly, I thought she was mentally unbalanced, but now..." he shrugged.

"Didn't the new cleaner notice?"

"About that time I had a bit of a fall. Broke my hip. Was in convalescence for six months. Then took a sabbatical for another six to fully recover. During that time, the rector from Upper Malby took over, but he didn't live here. The place was empty almost a year. When I returned I hired Mavis here in the village. Lovely woman, but nearly as old as I am. Still, she does an excellent job and she's never complained once."

Likely by the time Mavis had taken over, the body would have decomposed enough to stop smelling. She might have never noticed. Maybe a lingering odd odor she couldn't place, but nothing suspicious.

Lucas reentered the kitchen, tucking his cell phone away. "The police still can't get through. I've sent them pictures and a video and they're fairly certain we're correct about it being the curate, based on time frame. Since it's been there so long, they're not in a hurry." He glanced down at the vicar who'd buried his face in hands. Lucas lifted an eyebrow as if to ask if the vicar was okay. I nodded. "Anyway, we're to find you somewhere to stay," he said to the vicar, "and lock the place up tight until the crime scene investigators can get here and process the rectory."

The vicar nodded. "I can stay with Mavis. She has plenty of room and is a very good cook. Plus she lives just across the way so we can keep an eye on the place." He sighed heavily. "I suppose I should go pack."

"I'll come with you," Lucas said.

They disappeared down the hall and I could hear the low rumble of their voices as they climbed the stairs to the second floor. Poor vicar. I couldn't imagine how he must feel. I was certainly a little shaky.

I dialed Cheryl's number and waited until she answered sleepily. "Do you know what time it is?"

"Three in the morning?"

There was a pause. "Close. What's up? Did someone die?"

"You have a suspicious mind," I said. "But yes. Two someone's, actually." I quickly told her about Blodgett and about finding the curate.

"Only you would go on vacation and find a bunch of dead bodies. Leave it to the police, Viola."

"I would, except they're stuck on the other side of the flood."

She groaned. "Figures. Just be careful, okay?"

"I will. How are things back home?"

"Do you know what that Bat did to me?"

James "Bat" Battersea was Astoria's hottest police detective. And I mean that in both the looks and the ability department. Bat had been crushing on Cheryl as long as I'd known him, but Cheryl was either playing deliberately dumb, or she was just unaware. I'd never been sure which. Even a brief date during Valentine's Day hadn't straightened things out. I was beginning to think it would take a miracle.

"What did he do?" I asked, wondering if he'd finally made a declaration.

"He gave me a speeding ticket. Can you believe it?"

I hid a smirk, though I knew she couldn't see me. "Well, were you?"

"Was I what?" she asked.

"Were you speeding?"

Another pause. "That is *not* the point."

The kitchen door swung open and Jez popped her head in. "What's taking so long?"

"Cheryl, I gotta go. Call you later."

"You better. I want to know all the juicy details," she said.

I hung up and quickly told Jez what had happened. She let out a long whistle. "That's crazy. Why do you suppose Blodgett showed up here after all this time?"

"I'm not sure," I admitted. "Maybe he wanted to revisit the scene of the crime. Make sure the body was still hidden. Or re-hide it, even." I'd read about such things. Murders visiting the bodies they'd buried. Sometimes reburying them if they thought the police were closing in.

She plopped down in one of the empty chairs. "Think his murder has anything to do with this curate?"

"Probably," I said. "Otherwise it's quite the coincidence, and I don't believe in coincidences." Footsteps creaked overhead. I could make out the vicar's light step and Lucas's heavier one. I hoped they'd hurry up. I imagined the curate's body staring at me from the next room, even though there wasn't anything left to stare with.

"But who could have known Blodgett murdered the curate?" Jez asked. "Everyone thought the curate absconded with the silver. Which is silly, if you ask me. He'd have made more money staying a curate. Everyone knows that."

"That is a very good question," I admitted. One I didn't have an answer to. Yet.

Lucas returned with the vicar who was carrying a small overnight bag. "I'll walk you to Mavis's house," Lucas offered.

"Not necessary. It's just across the street."

We all stepped outside and the vicar locked up the rectory. As we walked toward the car a thought struck me. "By the way, what was the curate's full name?"

The vicar blinked. "Didn't I say? His name was Robin Carsley."

# # #

"Now isn't that interesting," I said as we waved goodbye to the reverend. "It can't possibly be a coincidence that a James Carsley is staying at a hotel less than a mile from where a Robbie Carsley's body was found. The very same hotel where the man who likely murdered Robin Carsley was also staying."

"No," Lucas agreed. "If it was a name like Smith, I'd buy it. But Carsley isn't that common."

"I wonder why Rupert didn't say anything." Jez said. "Surely he'd recognize Blodgett's name from the robbery."

"Good point," I agreed. "We should definitely confront him."

Lucas shot me a wry look. "Easy does it, Viola. You don't want to piss him off. There's only one hotel in this town and we're stuck there for the time being."

I heaved an exasperated sigh. He was, unfortunately, right. "Okay, I'll go easy on Rupert. But I'm not going easy on James. I saw him arguing with Blodgett just a couple hours before he was killed. And now we find out James has got the same last name as the curate Blodgett probably murdered ten years ago? He has some explaining to do. What if James Carsley is a relative and he killed Blodgett in revenge?"

"Oh, scandalous," Jez said with a grin. "But a bit of a stretch, don't you think? I mean, how would James know Blodgett killed Robin? If he's even related. Everyone believed the curate had run off."

"The family didn't. Father Thomas told me Robbie's relatives insisted he was innocent."

As we zipped through the village on our way back to the hotel, I had a thought. "We should go to the pub for dinner," I suggested. "Maybe Simon will have some more gossip. I'm surprised he didn't mention the curate when he was telling us all about that ghost woman."

"He might have if we hadn't left when we did. I have a feeling he had plenty of stories left to 'share' with us." Lucas turned on to the drive leading to the manor. "Dinner at the pub sounds good, though."

"I'll pass," said Jez. "I want to get a head start on ghost hunting."

#

"Thank goodness you're back." The minute we walked through the front door of the hotel, Rupert practically pounced on us. Today he was wearing navy blue cords and a cream cable knit sweater. His ring of graying hair was sticking up wildly as if hit with static electricity.

"What's the problem?" Lucas asked as he shrugged out of his charcoal pea coat. I always did like a man in a pea coat. Ridiculously sexy.

"Colonel Frampton is driving me bonkers," Rupert said, turning pleading eyes to Lucas. "He's a little *too* in his element, if you know what I mean. Can you please calm him down? He's already upset the poor Carsley's terribly."

"So, the police notified them about Robin Carsely?" I asked.

"Unfortunately, yes. James went on a tear. I thought he'd break everything in the drawing room, but then he went off and got drunk. Monica's been crying off and on for the last two hours." He turned back to Lucas. "Please. Frampton is just making things worse."

"I'll give it a shot," Lucas said.

As I unzipped my own jacket I asked, "Why didn't you mention you knew Jeffrey Blodgett?"

Rupert froze. "What do you mean?" His face had gone pale and a line of sweat popped out along his upper lip. He fidgeted a little as if he couldn't stand still.

"You had to have known he was involved in the theft at the church ten years ago," I said. It was a wild speculation, but I had a feeling in the pit of my stomach.

"I-I didn't realize it was the same man." A crimson flush crept up Rupert's neck and into his cheeks.

I gave him a look and Jez snorted with derision. It was clear he was lying.

"Fine," he hissed. "I knew it was him, but he served his time. What was I supposed to do about it? Throw him out on the streets? He was a paying guest."

"Ah, the almighty dollar," I said. "Or pound, rather. You didn't think to mention all this when he wound up dead with a letter opener in his back?"

Rupert shrugged. "I didn't see that it was important."

"You—." I literally spluttered in rage.

Lucas wrapped one arm around my shoulders and steered me away from Rupert. "I'm going to go have a chat with Colonel Frampton," he said in a low voice. "Why don't you put our coats away and then go have a chat with James Carsley. It would be very interesting to know if he is, as we suspect, related to the dead curate."

"I was planning on that," I snapped in annoyance. "Why don't *you* put the coats away?"

"Because you need to calm down before you confront Carsley. Otherwise you'll get his hackles up." He gave me a stern look, which was irritating. But he was right. I needed a breather because right now I felt like strangling Rupert.

"Fine," I snapped. I pulled away from him and turned to Jez. "You want to come with me?"

"Are you kidding?" She looked like a kid on Christmas. "Wild horses couldn't drag me away."

"All right, then. Let me put the coats in our room and I'll meet you back here in five minutes." I took the stairs two at a time, in a hurry to get on with it. I had a feeling James Carsley was in this up to his neck.

Shéa MacLeod

Chapter 9
The Beast and Bauble

Jez and I found James Carsley in the hotel bar. Apparently someone had let him in, and he was helping himself to an expensive looking whiskey. Not that I knew much about whiskey. I'm more of a blackberry bourbon girl myself, but Lucas was fond of the stuff and I recognized the label as one of the more pricey ones.

"Hi, James," I said, climbing onto a stool next to him. Jez sat on the other side of me, elbows on the bar. "I'm so sorry about Robin."

He slugged back a finger of whiskey and poured himself another. "Thanks. Robbie was a good kid." His tone was gruff and he didn't look at either of us.

"He was your brother?" I was guessing, but it seemed plausible.

"Yeah."

"I heard some stories about him down at the pub." I figured James would know what I was talking about and I was right. The muscles around his mouth tightened and he curved one hand into a fist.

"Those bastards should keep their mouths shut," he growled. He downed the glass of whiskey and reached to pour another. I stopped him by laying a hand over his, and giving him a friendly squeeze. I noticed he was trembling. I wondered if it was rage, fear, or something else entirely.

"Why didn't you tell Colonel Frampton why you're here? And about knowing Blodgett?" I asked.

"Because it's no one's business but mine," he snarled, yanking his hand from beneath mine as if I had the plague.

"Really?" I lifted a brow. "Because from where I'm sitting, you have a really good motive for murdering Blodgett."

"Is that so?" He stared into the empty glass.

"It's pretty likely that Blodgett killed your brother and walled him up in the rectory. Revenge is a strong motive."

He turned to glare at me. His nasty expression might have made a weaker woman quail, but I'd stared down murderers before. In fact, the last one I'd chased through the streets of Astoria. James Carsley wasn't about to scare me off.

"Not only do you have a motive, but I saw you arguing with Blodgett shortly before he died," I continued. "Believe me, you're the first person the police are going to look at."

"Well, I didn't do it. I had no idea Blodgett killed my brother. I didn't even know for sure Robbie was dead."

"Then what were you arguing about?" Jez asked soothingly, peering around my shoulder.

"You should tell us," I urged, keeping my tone as calm as possible. I was hoping the good-cop routine would work on him. "When the police get here, it'll be useful to have someone on your side."

He was silent so long I thought maybe he wasn't going to answer. Finally he blurted, "Fine. If you want to know, when we got the notification that Blodgett had been released, I came down here to clear my brother's name. I wanted to prove to the world he was innocent. I didn't expect him to be dead." He scrubbed a hand over his eyes, which were suspiciously wet. "I argued with Blodgett because I wanted him to admit the truth. That he'd committed the burglary on his own. That Robbie had nothing to do with the theft."

"And did he admit it?" I asked.

"No. He laughed in my face. Told me to get over it. Then he left the room. That's when I went upstairs and took a shower. I couldn't stand to be anywhere near him." He stood up so abruptly his stool toppled over with a loud clatter. "Now, if you're done being nosey, I've got better things to do." And with that he stomped out of the room, anger rolling off him in waves.

"What do you think?" Jez asked when he was gone.

"I think James Carsley is lying," I said. "He's still at the top of my suspect list."

# # #

The Beast and Bauble was warm and cheerful and busier than it had been the night before. Maybe because the weather was better. Or maybe because it was a Friday night. Probably because everyone was still stuck in the village thanks to flooding. In any case, I found a table in the back corner while Lucas went to get us drinks. I settled into the chair next to the window. The panes were steamed up so I couldn't see out. I perused the menu instead. I decided the steak and mushroom pie sounded delicious on a chill night. And if I had room, I was totally going for the sticky toffee pudding. I was on vacation after all.

Lucas soon returned with an Irish coffee for me and a straight up whiskey for himself. It reminded me of James Carsley downing whiskey in the hotel bar.

"I think I'll go with the chicken hot pot," he said. "It sounds wonderfully stodgy."

I felt a little guilty slipping out without asking Jez to come with us, but she'd said she wanted to ghost hunt and I wanted time alone with Lucas. Well, alone-ish, since we were surrounded by what looked like half the village.

When our food arrived I almost wished I'd gone with the chicken hot pot, too. Chicken breast over mashed potatoes smothered in cheese and some kind of sauce, what could be bad about that? Still, I tucked in, enjoying my steak and mushroom pie.

I took a sip of my drink. Bliss. Terry the barman really knew how to make an Irish coffee. "I know James Carsley has an alibi," I said over the rim of my mug. "But honestly? I'm suspicious. I mean, who else has such a great motive? And is there anyone to confirm his alibi? He was up there alone for what, twenty minutes at least? Could have easily slipped downstairs, stabbed Blodgett, and then run back upstairs, no one the wiser." Although no blood at the scene meant the body had been moved. I was still stuck on that.

"It's possible," Lucas agreed as he carefully cut a piece of chicken and scooped it up on his fork along with a healthy serving of potato. "It's so obvious, though, don't you think?" He popped the bite in his mouth and chewed slowly, a dimple flashing in his cheek. Curse the man, he even chewed sexily. How was that even possible?

"Sure," I said. "But that doesn't make him innocent."

"No," he admitted. "It does not. By the way, I asked Rupert about the letter opener."

"Yeah?"

"He claims it was always kept on the desk. Right out where anyone could see or take it."

"Interesting." I took another sip of Irish coffee before digging into my pie. "We should talk to Professor Huxton-Bennington. She was supposedly in the library. I wonder if she saw it."

"Good question."

The door swung open letting in a gust of wind and a spattering of rain drops. Goodie. It was raining again. Along with the wind and rain came a figure swathed in layers of coats and scarves as if it was freezing out instead of just a bit windy and damp. The figure took off his hat and I recognized him immediately.

"Look, its Simon. We should ask him about the theft and the curate. Maybe he knows something more."

"Good plan." Lucas waved the older man over.

At first Simon looked confused. No surprise since he'd been pretty drunk the night before. Then his expression cleared and a smile creased his weathered face.

"Sit down," Lucas said. "Let me get you a drink."

"Ah, if it isn't the young American ghost hunters. How are you this fine evening?" Simon took a seat at our table, face beaming, while Lucas got up to get him a pint from the bar.

It was neither a fine evening nor were we ghost hunters, but I didn't want to sidetrack the man. "Did you hear about the murder at the manor?" I asked.

"That I did. Quite shocking." He leaned forward so I could smell the booze on his breath. He'd obviously got started early. "Not that it's a surprise mind. Seeing as how it was Jeffrey Blodgett as got himself killed."

"You knew him?" That was a surprise.

"Met him a good ten years ago. Was on the construction crew what was fixing up the rectory. Some folks got their knickers in a twist about the new vicar updating the place. Saying he was too good for his station. Truth is the old vicar was cheap. Hadn't done a thing since the seventies, I reckon. Had to be done. Place was a wreck."

Lucas returned with the pint, which earned him effusive thanks from Simon. He took a long swallow of ale and set down his glass with a sigh.

"Blodgett," I prompted. "Why didn't you mention the theft when you were telling us about the ghost? Seems like a good story."

"Well, that was before we knew Blodgett killed poor Robbie Carsley, wasn't it? Didn't seem much of a tale."

"How did you meet him? Blodgett, I mean." I took another bite of pie, barely tasting it.

"Back then I did the gardening for the rectory and the church. The arthritis wasn't so bad then. Naturally I saw the workmen coming and going."

"How many were there?" Lucas asked.

Simon squinted. "Three. No four. That's right. They had a young boy with them helping out. Trainee or some such. They'd come to the pub in the evening before heading home." He took another sip of his ale. "Chatted with 'em a few times, but they was town folks. Not very chatty."

I wasn't sure how being town folks made them less chatty than other folks. "So, no one had any idea Blodgett murdered the curate? They really thought the curate ran off with the silver?"

"Aye that they did. The curate was an incomer, you see. He had a rough past, too. Trouble in his teens. Nobody really trusted him even though the vicar urged everyone to give him a chance. When he disappeared everyone figured they were right and the vicar was wrong."

"Did anyone look into the workmen?" Lucas asked.

"Police did. But there was no evidence and the only one as disappeared was Robbie Carsley. Case closed far as they were concerned."

We chatted a bit more with Simon, but didn't get anything else out of him except for another ghost story. This one about a ghost duck that disappeared into the hedgerows after causing cars to swerve into ditches. So we bid him goodnight and headed back up the road to the manor house. Hopefully tonight would be calm and uninterrupted. One body was quite enough.

Chapter 10
Pigs in Blankets

We arrived back at the hotel to find everyone gathered in the drawing room for an evening "tipple." Apparently post-dinner sherry was a thing. Rupert manned the sherry bottle pouring everyone a thimble full in dainty crystal glasses that probably cost a fortune. There was a platter of cheese and crackers set out on the coffee table and Bill was passing around a plate of canapes that looked like fancy pigs in blankets.

Marilyn Toppenish was still ensconced in her chair closest to the fire, though she'd put her knitting away in the gaudy tote bag she kept by her side. "Another, Rupert," she barked, thrusting her empty glass at him. With an exasperated sigh, Rupert complied. I noticed she not only had a small, china plate piled high with snacks, but her usual box of chocolates was open on the end table next to her. She clearly wasn't sharing.

"She really should be more careful," Jez muttered as she strolled up to me, half-empty sherry glass in hand. She shoved her glasses a bit farther up on her nose. "She's got diabetes, you know."

"Really? How do you know?"

"She told me. She's a bit of a talker," Jez said dryly.

She wasn't kidding. I'd experienced Marilyn's garrulousness myself. "Isn't it dangerous for her to drink alcohol and eat chocolates?"

Jez shrugged. "Depends on how well under control it is. With insulin and a careful diet, she could eat or drink a small amount. Unfortunately, from what I've seen, Marilyn has a terrible diet and she's constantly eating those chocolates. She's gone through three boxes in the last two days."

"Maybe she's just going a little crazy because she's on vacation." I'd been known to overindulge a time or two myself. Visions of sticky toffee pudding danced in my head.

"Maybe," Jez admitted. "But it's super dangerous. And an ambulance wouldn't be able to get through if something went wrong."

Scary thought. I hadn't really considered that aspect of being trapped. I was more concerned with the police and the dead body in Rupert's refrigerator. Not to mention the remains of Robbie Carsley still half plastered behind the rectory wall.

"How'd the ghost hunting go?" I asked, forcing my overactive imagination away from the crime scene.

"Nothing yet," she said cheerfully, "but it's early." She polished off the rest of her sherry. "I'm going to take a quick cat nap and then do another pass around midnight. Join me? It could be fun."

The thought of that creepy attic at night made me shiver. "No thanks. I like my beauty sleep."

"Suit yourself. 'Night." Jez wandered out of the room. No one bid her goodnight.

James and Monica Carsley were once again in their places on the sofa under the window. They sat as far apart as they could without looking like they were avoiding each other. James had eschewed sherry in favor of beer, which he was drinking straight out of the bottle, much to Rupert's disgust. Monica had barely touched her sherry. She looked wan and had dark circles under her eyes. I wondered if she'd been sleeping and how the news of Robbie's death had affected her. Had she even known him? I made a mental note to get Monica alone and ask about her marriage and her brother-in-law.

Lucas was having a chat with the Colonel in the far corner. Their voices were a low rumble and every now and then the Colonel would glance at somebody or other, his thick eyebrows beetled with suspicion.

Bill had set aside the canapés and was fiddling with the lights using his cell phone. Personally, I thought it was kind of cool that he could control the dimmer switch with an app, but Marilyn wasn't having it. Every time he'd change the settings, she'd snarl at him, "Do you mind? I'm trying to knit." With the amount of alcohol she'd consumed, I was surprised she could hold the needles.

Lavender Wu was dressed in the same clothes she'd arrived in. They were a little more crumpled than before, but her hair and makeup were flawless. Between pages of her book, she cast hungry glances at Lucas. I was torn between laughing at her and punching her in the face.

I noticed Professor Huxton-Barrington and her husband were at the gaming table again. This time playing cribbage. I decided it was as good a time as any to ask the professor about the letter opener.

"Professor," I said cheerfully, pulling up a chair to the gaming table. "Mr. Huxston-Barrington."

"Oh, call me Martin," he said with a charming smile.

"Martin, then. I'm Viola." I turned to the professor. "May I call you Abigail?"

"No."

All righty then. I gave her a tight smile. "Professor, I have a question for you. About the letter opener."

Her expression was cold, disinterested. Her slightly protuberant eyes remained fixed on her cards. "You mean the murder weapon."

"Yes," I admitted. "You see, I noticed it when I was in the library earlier. Rupert says it was always kept out on the desk. Easily available to anyone passing by. I wondered, when you were in the room, did you notice if the letter opener was on the desk?"

"Actually, I know it wasn't." She counted her hand and moved her peg along the board. "I needed it to take a staple out of some paperwork for a class I'm teaching next month, and I couldn't find it. It wasn't on the desk or in the drawer. I even looked underneath the desk just in case someone might have knocked it off. It wasn't there."

"So the killer must have taken it before you entered the room," I said.

She seemed to visibly relax, as if realizing the letter opener going missing before she got there spoke to her innocence. "I would say so, yes."

"You see, dear," Martin said, patting her pale hand. "You can't possibly be a suspect."

I didn't bother to point out that she wasn't exactly cleared. After all, it was easy enough to lie, but she seemed to be telling the truth. And I couldn't see how or why she would kill Blodgett.

"Is there anything else?" she asked in her carefully enunciated tones.

"No. Thanks. You've helped a lot." I stood up. "Did you ever get the staple out?"

She lifted an eyebrow. "Pardon?"

"Just curious if you managed to get the staple out. Since you couldn't find the letter opener." I gave her a vacant smile. Nobody home here. Just asking stupid questions.

"I did, actually," she admitted. "I used my nail file."

"How clever."

"Indeed." She narrowed her eyes. Apparently my guileless act wasn't fooling her.

I strolled over to the window. Outside it was already dark. Rain pattered against the windows, lighter now as if the early downpour had worn itself out.

"Learn anything interesting?" I asked Lucas as he joined me. He wrapped a warm arm around my shoulders and bent his head closer to mine.

"Unfortunately, no. The colonel was more interested in reminiscing about his time in Africa than about the matter at hand. You?"

"The professor claims that when she arrived in the library, the letter opener wasn't there. It was very definitely there earlier, so someone must have taken it sometime between when I observed the argument between Blodgett and Carsley, and nine-twenty when the professor arrived in the library."

"Interesting," Lucas said thoughtfully. "Which means whoever killed Blodgett had to have already planned to kill him with the letter opener."

"Exactly. And there's just one person it could have been."

Lucas lifted an eyebrow. "Oh?"

I gave him a wolfish smile. "James Carsley."

Chapter 11
The Body At Breakfast

Tracking down James Carsley was easier said than done. By the time I realized he had to have taken the letter opener, he and Monica had already left the drawing room.

"I believe they went upstairs," Rupert said apologetically. "You may have to wait until the morning."

"This can't wait," I snapped. We were about to solve a murder, for crying out loud!

Lucas collected the colonel and explained the situation. Colonel Frampton was surprised to say the least. "Are you certain? He has an alibi."

"His alibi is that he was in the shower. Not exactly iron clad," I said sarcastically.

The colonel let out a harrumph. "Very well. Let us see what he has to say for himself."

The three of us tromped upstairs. I could hear the murmurings of the rest of the group as they gathered at the bottom of the stairs, unwilling to be left out entirely. Lucas hammered on the door to the Carsley's room. The door swung open immediately revealing Monica already in her robe. It was terry cloth, like mine at home, well-worn and graying. Hers had a faded pink heart on one pocket. It added twenty pounds to her slender frame. Maybe it was time to throw mine away.

"Can I help you?" she asked in a timid voice. Her wide eyes were a surprisingly lovely shade of whisky-gold, rimmed by naturally dark lashes. It struck me that she must have been quite pretty five or so years ago.

"Is your husband in?" Colonel Frampton asked in a booming voice, causing Monica to flinch. I suspected he was hard of hearing. He always seemed to talk so loud.

"No. I'm sorry. He isn't." She fiddled with the collar of her robe, her fingers nervously twitching the fabric.

"Dear lady, I must speak with your husband *immediately*. Have you any idea where he is?" Frampton asked.

"He didn't say. He just...stormed out. We had a little argument." Her cheeks flushed and she cast her gaze to the floor.

"About what?" Lucas asked gently.

"I think he's having an affair," she admitted in a tear-choked voice. "He's been behaving oddly lately. I finally had enough and asked him. He got angry with me, said I was an idiot, and stormed out."

"I'm really sorry," I said soothingly. "That's awful. But do you have any idea where he might have gone?"

She shrugged. "Bar, probably. Or the pub in the village. He does like his drink."

"Monica, did you ever meet your brother-in-law, Robbie?" I asked.

She shook her head. "James and I only met eight years ago."

We thanked her and headed downstairs to the bar. At the foot of the stairs everyone else scattered, pretending they hadn't been eavesdropping the entire time. Jez—who had returned from wherever she'd wandered off—gave me a thumbs up. Marilyn gave me a knowing look. Only Lavender seemed completely bored by the whole thing.

Sure enough, James was perched on a bar stool. He'd helped himself to a bottle of scotch and was doing it justice. He was definitely tipsy already.

"We need to have a word with you, young man," the colonel boomed.

Carsley didn't even look up. He tossed back a finger of scotch and poured himself another.

"You killed Blodgett, didn't you?" I blurted.

He flinched. "Don't know where you got that idea."

"When I was in the library during your argument with Blodgett shortly before nine o'clock, the letter opener was on the desk. However, when Professor Huxton-Barrington arrived at twenty minutes past nine, it was gone. The next time anyone saw it was when I found it lodged in Blodgett's back." I eyed him closely, waiting for his reaction.

"So?" But he didn't look at me.

"So, you're the only one who could have taken it," I said. "Here's what I think. You never believed Robbie ran off with the stolen goods from St. Oswins, did you?"

"Of course not," he snapped. "Robbie was a good person. The best. He would never do that. Sure, he got into some trouble as a kid, but he grew out of that."

"If Robbie didn't steal anything, he'd have no reason to run," I reasoned. "And if he didn't run, then he must still be in Chipping Poggs. You suspected all along he was dead. Didn't you?"

"I know it," he slurred. "Knew it from the very first."

"And when they arrested Blodgett nine years ago, you knew he was the one who killed Robbie. Maybe you visited him in prison. Maybe he wouldn't see you. Maybe you just tried to get on with your life. But then you got the news Blodgett had been let out early on good behavior." I was on a roll. The colonel appeared baffled. Lucas just watched in amusement.

James snorted. "As if. That bastard should have been locked away for good."

"Except he wasn't. He was free and your brother was lying dead somewhere only Blodgett knew about. So you tracked him down. How did you discover he was here?"

James laughed. "Idiot posted it on social media."

That was about the dumbest criminal move I'd ever heard of. "You decided to come down here. Confront Blodgett. Maybe even get him to admit to killing Robbie and telling you where the body was buried. But Blodgett was too smart. He had no intention of going to prison for murder. And besides, he was kind of a jerk, so he probably didn't feel the slightest bit guilty."

"Kind of a jerk?" James scoffed. "The man was a world class wanker."

"Ladies present," barked the colonel.

I'd heard worse. I waved him off and continued. "You confronted Blodgett in the study. The two of you argued and he left. You saw the letter opener and decided if you couldn't have justice, you could have revenge. So, you stabbed him in the back. Job done."

"It wasn't like that," he snapped.

"Then what was it like?" I asked.

"I was just...so angry. It was like a red haze came over me. I didn't know what I was doing until it was all over."

I wasn't sure I bought that. On the one hand it was believable. If I knew someone had offed my sister and then taunted me about it, I'd probably do something stupid, too. But stabbing someone in the back hours after an argument? "He deserved it. Don't tell me he didn't." James was sputtering in anger now.

"I won't," I agreed. "But it's still wrong. You should have let the police handle it."

"Maybe," he admitted. "But I had no idea Robbie's body was going to turn up, did I? I figured no one would ever know what happened unless I did something."

"James Carsley, you're under citizen's arrest for murder." The colonel stood up straight and tall like he was addressing his troops. "The police will be here in the morning. I shall turn you over to them along with all evidence gleaned from this investigation."

"Fine," James said. He didn't look up, just poured another scotch. "I know the truth. That's all that matters."

"We'll need to lock him up," Lucas pointed out. "We can't let him roam around freely like nothing happened."

"There are some storage rooms in the attic," I said. "Some of them have only tiny windows. We could put a cot in one of them and lock him in."

"Good plan," Lucas agreed.

The colonel was also in agreement. So, Bill and Rupert set up a temporary holding cell in the attic and the colonel locked James Carsley in for the night. Carsley didn't even protest, though Monica started crying so hard that Lavender Wu ended up giving her a lorazepam.

The rest of the night passed quietly. I was kind of looking forward to turning this whole thing over to the police and getting on with our vacation. Frankly, I'd had enough of death.

Still, something niggled at the back of my brain. Something made me just a little uneasy.

#

The next morning dawned to more torrential rain, which only increased the flooding. Added to that was the news that the police were still unable to get through.

"You'd think they'd send somebody in a boat or something," I muttered to Lucas. "Not only do we have two dead bodies, but we've got a killer locked up, as well."

"They'll come when they can. No doubt there are a lot of people in dire straits out there who need their help. We're fine here for now. The murderer is locked up tight." Lucas handed me a cup of coffee heavily doctored with milk and sugar. I wrinkled my nose. What I wouldn't give for proper cream.

I gazed around the room. The professor was sitting at a table near the window sipping a cup of tea and tapping away on a tablet. Martin was up at the sideboard slapping strawberry jam on a buttered crumpet. Otherwise the room was empty.

Lavender Wu appeared in the doorway, posed dramatically, and glared at everyone. She was still wearing the pants from her suit, but had left off the jacket. She strode toward the coffee urn perched on the buffet. She reached it just as Martin turned around, plate in hand, and ran straight into her. His freshly made crumpet went jam-first right into her white blouse. Lavender leapt backward with a cry.

"You idiot! You've ruined my blouse. Do you have any idea how much this cost?"

While Martin babbled apologies and offered to have her blouse cleaned, I sat staring at the large, red stain across her chest. The niggle in my brain from the night before turned into a full alarm bell clanging away wildly.

Lavender caught me staring and whipped around with a glare that would have made the queen herself quail. "What are you staring at?"

I gave her a slow smile that, if she'd have known me, would have made her just a little afraid. "Nothing. Nothing at all." Then I grabbed Lucas by the arm and hissed, "Follow me."

He followed me dutifully out into the hall, leaving his half eaten breakfast on the table. "This better be good," he muttered. "I didn't eat my bacon yet."

"Forget your bacon. This is better. Where's that fridge where you stuck Blodgett's body?"

"Why?"

I tapped my foot impatiently.

He sighed. "Fine. This way."

He led the way into the kitchen where Bill was frying up eggs. "Something wrong with brekkie, mate?" he asked, a frown line marring his smooth forehead.

"It was delicious," Lucas assured him. "Viola just wanted me to look at something. Then I plan to finish it." He shot me a stern look.

"Whatever. Show me the body."

"Don't think you're supposed to be in there," Bill said. "The colonel was quite insistent."

"It's important," I said, swinging the heavy door open. I stepped inside only to be assaulted by a gust of cold air that chilled me straight to my bones. I was going to need a lot more hot coffee after this.

Blodgett's body was wrapped in a white sheet and lying on the floor of the walk-in refrigerator. I hunched down beside him and lifted the sheet, using the flashlight on my phone to light up the side of Blodgett's throat. "Bingo."

"What is it?" Lucas stepped up beside me and stared down at the body. "That's interesting."

"Isn't it just." I pulled the sheet lower revealing the letter opener still stuck in the dead man's back. I carefully inspected the wound without touching anything. "Just as I thought." I re-covered the body and we both left the fridge.

"Let's go find the colonel," Lucas suggested, apparently forgetting his uneaten bacon.

I nodded. "Good plan."

We found Colonel Frampton reading a two-day-old newspaper and sipping a cup of tea in the drawing room. Other than him, it was empty, Marilyn Toppenish having yet to put in an appearance.

"Colonel, we have a problem," I said without preamble.

He carefully laid his paper aside and removed his reading glasses. "Problem?"

"The stab wound didn't kill Jeffrey Blodgett."

He lifted one white brow. "Pardon?"

I sat down on the chair facing him and leaned forward. "You see, it was the jam."

He looked utterly confused. "I'm afraid you'll have to explain."

"Something's been bothering me about this murder. I just couldn't put my finger on it. Then this morning Martin Huxton-Barrington was carrying a crumpet with strawberry jam. He ran smack into Lavender Wu and got red jam all over her clean, white shirt. And that's when it hit me."

The colonel rubbed his forehead tiredly. "I still don't follow."

"When I found Jeffrey Blodgett, there was hardly any blood. The letter opener blade had to be at least six inches long. There should have been blood everywhere. At the very least, quite a bit of it around the wound. Possibly even some on the floor beneath him."

The colonel was nodding. "Agreed. I've seen it myself on the battlefield."

"Right, but there wasn't any."

"I thought the body was moved."

"Which would explain the lack of blood on the floor, but not the lack of blood on the wound." I watched him closely as the mist cleared. It was his turn to lean forward. His eyes glowed with excitement.

"Do you mean to tell me the man was dead *before* he was stabbed?"

"That's what we think, sir," said Lucas. He squeezed my shoulder. "There were bruises around his neck. Somebody strangled and killed him before he was stabbed. Perhaps twenty minutes or more."

"Then—."

"Then James Carsley is innocent," I said. "Someone else killed Blodgett."

Chapter 12
Haunted By the Ghost

I was half afraid James was going to sue us for false arrest or kidnapping or something—which was how Lucas and I convinced the colonel to let him out—but he was so relieved he actually hugged the colonel. The colonel got a little blustery and gruff and told James to man up. Fortunately, James ignored him.

Monica cried all over James. He was kinder to her than I'd ever seen him. In fact, he looked...lighter somehow. As if the weight of being a murder suspect had somehow lightened the load of his need for revenge.

"I'm so relieved," he said. "I really thought I'd killed him. I wanted him to pay for murdering my brother, but—." He shook his head. "I'm glad I didn't do it."

"Will the police charge him?" I asked Lucas later over lunch. Rupert had steered us toward the sweet little tea room not far from St. Oswins. It was in a four hundred year old thatched cottage. The sign outside had an image of a Victorian lady's boot with the inscription: "The Wrinkled Stocking: Cream Teas served."

Inside, a fire burned in a woodstove set into the large fireplace. It made the room nice and toasty. Half a dozen little tables with white cotton cloths and mix-matched china settings were crammed into the room. The owner was a tall, raw-boned woman with clever eyes and heavy lines around her mouth marking her as a former smoker.

She looked out of place in the delicate shop. I recognized her immediately as the woman with the yellow raincoat and green boots who'd give us directions the day we arrived in Chipping Poggs.

She introduced herself as Doris Simms and offered a menu with a stunning array of sandwiches, quiches, scones, and other delightful bits. "I bake everything myself," she said with pride. Lucas and I ordered a full afternoon tea complete with sandwiches and cakes.

Murder might be a rather macabre conversation to have over tea, but the place was so warm and cozy and the food so delicious, I felt removed from the horror. Now I was worried about James Carsley. I didn't want to see an innocent man pay for something he didn't do.

"They won't charge him with murder," Lucas assured me. "Maybe violating a dead body or tampering with evidence, but likely they'll let him go with a warning. It's clear he's remorseful. I'm sure they'll be understanding of his grief. Who wouldn't go a little crazy after being confronted with their brother's killer?" There was something in his tone.

"You never talk about your family," I said as I spread homemade strawberry jam and clotted cream over a fresh baked scone.

"Not much to tell." He focused on his turkey and cranberry tea sandwich.

"You seem to understand what James is going through," I pushed the issue. He was my boyfriend, for goodness sake. He should be able to share these things with me.

He set down his sandwich without taking a bite. "Anyone can have sympathy for another human being in pain."

"Bull," I snapped, irritated at his avoidance of the issue. "This is personal for you."

"I assure you, my brother is quite alive."

"But—."

"Can't we just let this drop?" He sounded tired.

I gave him a long look. Finally I said, "Why is it that I'm supposed to share my life with you? My innermost secrets? To let you in on my investigations and my hopes and dreams and everything in between? You get angry with me when I don't share. When I do my own thing. But when it comes to you and your past? Nothing. We don't talk about you. You get to hide whatever part of yourself you want. I mean look at you and the whole Israeli army thing. How long were we dating before you spilled that little gem? Well, forget it."

I stood up, threw my napkin down, and marched from the tea shop. I was so mad I yanked open the door a little too hard and wacked myself in the forehead. I stormed out as fast as I could not wanting him to see me cry. Because I wasn't sure he'd believe it was from the pain in my head.

# # #

After shooting a quick message to Cheryl ranting about idiot men, I spent the rest of the day ghost hunting with Jez at St. Oswin's. She assured me that while spotting a ghost was highly unlikely in the middle of the day, she wanted to get some good readings and images so she could come back after dark. "I need a baseline," she explained. "If you've got something to compare your readings to, it makes for more impressive evidence."

"Sure. Makes sense." I didn't tell her I was avoiding Lucas. I was a little embarrassed over my outburst and had the insanely strong urge to go apologize. At the same time I knew I wasn't entirely wrong and I needed him to acknowledge that.

The church was poorly heated and at least ten degrees cooler inside than out. I shivered in my jacket, wishing I had something heavier. Jez had me hold one of her gadgets and follow her around with the orders to notify her if I got any interesting readings. There weren't. I was bored out of my skull.

At some point, after what seemed like hours, the vicar entered the church. "Oh! You're still here."

"Sorry, Father," Jez said cheerfully. She glanced at the clock on her phone. "Is that the time? I lost track. My work is always so fascinating."

That was one word for it. Not the word I'd use, though.

"I'm afraid I need to set up for tonight's service. We're having a small memorial for Curate Carsley. Ease his way off to heaven."

If the curate was in heaven, he'd entered it quite some time ago. Still, I bit my tongue. These people probably needed some closure. A sense of normalcy. Who was I to spoil that for them?

"I hear his brother, James, killed that ghastly man up at the manor," Father Thomas said as he began lighting candles up on the altar.

"Actually," I said, "he didn't. I mean, he did stab Blodgett, but it turns out Blodgett was already dead. Somebody strangled him earlier. James thought Blodgett was sleeping and stabbed him."

"Oh, my. How shocking."

I eyed the vicar. He was a small man, and frail. It was hard to imagine him killing anyone. But could he have slipped into the manor without anyone noticing and strangled Jeffrey Blodgett? Unlikely, unless he was stronger than he looked. And why would he do it? He hadn't known at the time that the curate was dead. And surely he wouldn't kill over the stolen goods. Although I'd heard of murders being committed over less, I couldn't wrap my head around a vicar doing such a thing. Still, I mentally added him to my list of suspects.

It was getting dark outside and had started raining again, but this time it was a mere drizzle. "Don't worry," Jez said cheerfully. "I've got my brolly."

"Your what?"

She pulled a bright red umbrella out of her backpack. "It's what the British call their umbrellas. Don't you love it? Why don't we have a nickname for the things? Umbrella is such an unwieldy word, don't you think?"

I blinked. The girl could talk for Texas. Frankly all I wanted was a hot shower and a bed. But the idea of sleeping next to Lucas when I wanted to wring his neck was anything but restful. My stomach let out an unholy growl.

"Let's grab something to eat at the pub," Jez suggested. "It'll be quicker than going back to the hotel."

"Sure." Why not? I figured I should text Lucas so he wouldn't worry. I might be mad at him, but I wasn't a jerk. He replied with one word: *Fine.* I scowled at my phone screen. I might not be a jerk, but someone in this relationship sure was.

After a quick dinner of soup and sandwiches in the warmth of the pub, we walked back to the church. The congregation was just filtering out, and the vicar let us in before heading off to Mavis's house.

"They say midnight is the best time for ghosts," Jez informed me as she set up her equipment inside. "Truth is, ghosts are around all the time, so it doesn't really matter. Easier to spot variances in the dark, though. So, this is good. You heard the story of that poor woman that killed herself back in the day?"

"Mattie Doon? Sure. Simon, one of the old guys at the pub, told us when we first arrived." I remembered his story of the old woman who spotted Mattie's ghost ten years ago while she was out walking her dog. I still wondered if the ghost spotting had anything to do with the curate's murder. Maybe Mrs. Tillicum hadn't seen a ghost at all, but Blodgett hiding Robbie Carsley's body. Interesting.

"Well, I'd like to get in touch with Mattie," Jez was saying. "Can you imagine if she answered?"

"Uh, sure. Pretty exciting."

"You better believe it." She fiddled a little more with the camera she'd set up on a tripod. "Okay, ready. You stand here." She dragged me to a spot behind the camera and handed me the same device she had me use before. "It's on. No need to do anything. Just let me know if you get any interesting readings. Ready?"

"As I'll ever be."

She grinned, a dimple flashing in her left cheek. "Then let's do this thing." She spun around, clutching some other gadget that had all kinds of lights and dials on it. "Mattie Doon," she shouted. "Show yourself!"

I wasn't sure that was how one got a ghost to appear. I mean, if I were a ghost, I'd be pretty pissed if some idiot ran around yelling at me. But this was Jez's show, so I let her shout away.

An hour later Mattie hadn't shown herself and Jez was hoarse.

"Maybe we should try another ghost," I suggested. I had an inspiration. "What about Robbie Carsley?"

"The curate? Wasn't he found in the rectory?"

"Sure. But we're pretty sure he caught Blodgett stealing, so he was probably killed in or near the church, then dragged to the rectory."

She tapped her chin thoughtfully. "It might work. I mean, if he died on the grounds..." she spun around and started bellowing Robbie's name. Another hour ticked by and still nothing. Which didn't surprise me. I was relieved when she finally gave up.

"I guess we should head back to the hotel," she said, her expression crestfallen. "It's getting late. I can come back tomorrow."

I helped her pack up her gear and we drove back to the hotel. Lights streamed from the mullioned windows like beacons in the dark. It looked so cheerful and welcoming, yet inside lurked a cold blooded killer.

Chapter 13
Suddenly A Scream

Rupert was in the middle of serving sherry when Jez and I arrived back at the hotel. Jez took her gear upstairs and I wandered into the drawing room. I could use a glass of sherry. Or twelve.

I ignored Lucas, which wasn't easy. He was looking particularly tasty in soft, worn jeans and a snug heather gray Henley. Lavender Wu stood nearby eyeballing him like he was a chocolate cupcake and tossing her hair. If she wasn't careful she was going to give herself a neck spasm.

The only empty seat was near Marilyn, so I sank down into the cozy armchair and took the glass of sherry Rupert offered me. It was strong, sweet, and a touch fruity. I could get used to this.

"You've been ghost hunting with that other American, I hear," Marilyn said, giving me a knowing look.

"Seemed like something to do since we're more or less trapped here."

"I would think," she said, "that you'd be more interested in solving the crime."

I lifted an eyebrow. "What do you mean?" Surely she hadn't heard of my penchant for getting involved in murder investigations. It wasn't like I'd been in any major papers or anything. Maybe the odd internet blog post.

"You seemed to enjoy questioning everyone. Finding clues."

"Oh. Well. I read a lot of Agatha Christie." And watched a lot of *Murder, She Wrote*.

"I see you've cleared Carsley."

"Yeah. Blodgett was already dead when James stabbed him. Hard to get around the facts."

"It is, isn't it?" She gave me a meaningful look as she popped one of her chocolates in her mouth and chewed slowly. She didn't offer me one, which I thought was rude. I could use some chocolate. Maybe I'd sneak some later, though she'd likely notice.

"Do you know something, Marilyn? Something you didn't tell us about the murder?"

"Maybe I did. Maybe I didn't." She selected another chocolate.

I leaned forward. "If you know something, you need to tell us."

Her eyes narrowed. "I don't need to do any such thing. I will tell the police when they get here."

"Marilyn—."

She ignored me and held up her glass for a refill. Rupert obliged and she downed it in one gulp.

I sighed. "Marilyn, you could be putting your life at risk. What if the killer knows that you have information and decides to…"

"What? Silence me? Good luck to him." Her laugh was more than a little creepy.

#

I sat bolt upright in bed. According to my phone it was past two in the morning. Something woke me from a dead sleep, but I couldn't figure out what. Lucas was already reaching for his robe. A scream rent the air.

Without a word, Lucas flung open the door and charged down the hall with me hot on his heels. I didn't even bother wasting time on a robe. Though the minute I left the room I wished I had. The hall was chilly.

"It's Marilyn's room," I said. Her door was standing wide open and a shadowy figure stood in the doorway. I realized it was Jez, her face deathly pale.

"Sh-she's dead," she stammered. "S-sorry I screamed."

Lucas eased her out of the doorway and toward me. I steered her toward one of the antique benches that lined the hallway then went to join Lucas. No way was I being left out of this.

The layout of Marilyn's room was almost identical to ours except it lacked a bay window and the color scheme was burgundy and tan. She also appeared to be less organized than either Lucas or myself. There was clothing strewn everywhere around the room. The desk had been turned into a vanity of sorts with enough bottles, tubes, and pots to supply a makeup store. Her knitting bag had been dropped in the middle of one of the armchairs next to the fireplace. And in the center of the queen size bed lay Marilyn Toppenish.

She lay curled in on herself like she'd been in pain. Her eyes stared glassily into nothing. There was a trail of vomit from her mouth, down the side of the bed, and to a pool on the floor. The stench was almost overwhelming.

"What's going on here?" Colonel Frampton boomed from the doorway. Voices echoed down the hall. Great. We were going to have a crowd in a moment.

Lucas turned to address the colonel. "It's Marilyn. She's dead. Looks like she's maybe been poisoned."

The colonel closed his eyes a moment as if drawing strength. Then he opened them and, after closing the door firmly, strode toward the bed with a determined expression. "The rest of the guests do not need to see this. The poor woman. Yes, it does appear poison was the method, was it not? Who found her?"

"I did." Jez raised her hand. "Her door was open…"

"There now," the colonel clucked, giving her an awkward pat on the back. The man wasn't exactly stellar at comforting those in shock.

"How do you suppose the poison was administered?" Lucas mused.

"Could it have been in the sherry?" I asked. "It's pretty strong. It would mask the flavor of just about anything."

The colonel glanced at me. "We all drank the sherry."

"Someone could have slipped it in just her glass."

"Unlikely," Lucas said. "I watched Rupert pour the first glass and hand it to her. You were there for the other glasses." Of which there'd been many. No one but Rupert and Marilyn had touched her glass and there'd been no time for Rupert to slip anything into it.

"Fine. Not in the sherry then." I mulled it over. "She was diabetic. That could have been how the killer got her. Put the poison in her hypodermic. She administers it to herself. Dead a few hours later."

"It's a possibility," the colonel said grimly. "We'll have to find her latest needle. It may tell us something. But first I need to ring the police."

"You think they can get through?" Lucas asked.

"I hope so, dear boy. Our situation is getting rather dire."

Lucas offered his cell phone and the colonel put in a call to the local constabulary. Less than five minutes later he handed Lucas back the phone. "They're still stuck. We'll have to move the body into the refrigeration unit and lock up this room."

Great. The bodies were piling up, we had a killer on the loose, and the police couldn't get here until who knew when. I wandered over to the desk. Behind all the bottles and tubes was a red plastic bin with a snap top. It had the bio waste symbol in black on the side. I grabbed a tissue from a box on the vanity and used it to cover my hand while I popped open the top. I didn't want to get my fingerprints all over it. Inside were eight discarded needles. About two days' worth.

"I found her used needles." The overhead light was dim, so I used my phone flashlight to better illuminate the box. They all looked normal, with a residue of clear liquid except for the one on the very top. The liquid residue had a blueish-green tinge. "Found it. Looks a lot like antifreeze."

Lucas and the colonel walked over and peered in the box. "Excellent work," the colonel said.

"Maybe." I frowned. "Marilyn's been a diabetic for years."

The colonel appeared confused. "So?"

"She would have noticed if her insulin had changed color," Lucas said. "She would never have injected herself."

"Perhaps the killer injected her." The colonel seemed proud of his deduction.

"Wouldn't she have woken up?" I said.

"Maybe she did and it was too late," the colonel said.

Lucas shook his head. "Antifreeze takes a while to act. As much as twenty-four hours, depending on size and health of the person. It had to have been administered much earlier. I'm guessing the killer administered it some other way. Once Marilyn was asleep, he or she slipped back in and left the empty syringe, hoping the police would think she'd done it to herself."

"We need to figure out how she was poisoned," I muttered.

"We can do that later," the colonel said. "Right now we must remove the body for safe keeping."

While Lucas roped Bill into helping him move the body, Colonel Frampton tracked down Rupert and asked him to herd everyone into the drawing room.

"I suggest the dining room instead," Rupert said. "Everyone could use a hot cup of tea about now."

The colonel let out an exasperated sigh. I could tell he was about to argue, so I blurted out, "Great idea, Bill."

The colonel muttered a few choice words about interfering women. I ignored him.

With the body delivered to the refrigerator and the crime scene shut and locked, we marched into the dining room. We must have entered more noisily than I realized because all eyes swung toward us. The colonel cleared his throat.

"Ladies and gentlemen, your attention, please. I have some very bad news, I'm afraid." He cleared his throat again.

"Don't tell me I'm stuck in this hell hole another day," Lavender said waspishly. "I have things to do."

"You're not the only one, dearie." Professor Huxton-Barrington's tone was equally acidic. "Some of us are tired of hearing you whine."

Lavender glowered at her. "Oh, yeah—."

"Ladies!" The colonel held up his hands placatingly. "Please. This is not about the weather or the roads. I'm afraid to say, last night..." he trailed off as if afraid of saying it out loud.

"Last night," I continued for him, "Marilyn Toppenish was murdered."

Shéa MacLeod

Chapter 14
Chocolate and Bacon

There were several gasps and shocked cries of, "Oh, my god" and "What the devil?" Jez looked at me with wide eyes in a pale face, her pale pink mouth forming a perfect "o."

"Are you sure?" she asked.

"Dead sure." I winced at my word choice. "I mean, yes. We're sure."

"How?" Martin Huxton-Barrington asked. "How was she…killed?"

"Poison," the colonel offered.

The professor clutched at her proverbial pearls, her less-than-ample bosom heaving dramatically. "The sherry!"

"Don't be ridiculous," Jez snapped at her. "We all drank the sherry. If it had been poisoned, it would look like Jonestown in here."

I thought the professor might faint, but she was made of sterner stuff. She glared at Jez. "What an uncouth young woman you are."

"At least I'm not a drama queen," Jez snarled.

"It must have been something she ate," I interrupted the babble. "Did anyone see what she had for dinner last night?"

"She was in the bar," Rupert offered. "She had a shepherd's pie, two glasses of wine, and berry crumble for dessert."

"And don't forget stuffed mushrooms for starters," Lavender said. We all stared at her. She gave us a cool look, her thin lips slightly pursed. "What? I was sitting at the table next to her. And she didn't have one serving of crumble, she had three."

"Was it the food?" Monica asked, her pale face creased with worry. She was fiddling nervously with her collar again. The poor cardigan would never be the same again. Not that it was any loss. The thing looked like a mushroom.

"Let's see. Were the pies indivually cooked?" I turned to Bill.

"No," Bill said. "I made one large dish and served slices as it was ordered."

"Did anyone else have shepherd's pie last night?" I asked.

"I did." James Carsley stood up. "So did my wife." He laid his hand protectively on her shoulder.

"So did I," said Colonel Frampton.

"So, we know it wasn't the pie. Otherwise the rest of you would have been sick. Or worse." I sat down and rubbed my temple. Monica let out a strangled sob, which I ignored. "Mushrooms? Anyone have those?"

"I ate three while cooking." Bill flushed as Rupert shot him a glare. "I was hungry. Anka had them, too."

"We had them, as well," said Martin.

"Not the mushrooms then," I said. "What about the wine?"

"It was a red cab," Rupert offered. "I served it myself. Ms. Wu had a glass from the same bottle, as did Lucas."

Lucas nodded. "That's right. It was excellent wine."

"What about her glass?" I asked.

"Her glass was pristine. And it's unlikely anything was dropped in after I poured. The bar was quite busy for dinner service last night, but I took the glass straight out to her."

"I guess that brings us to the dessert." I glanced around. Everyone's hands were raised.

"I only make one dessert per night," Bill said. "It was served with custard."

"Sorry I missed that," I muttered. Lucas just looked smug, drat him.

"It clearly was not anything she ate at dinner," the colonel pointed out needlessly.

I paced the floor, tapping my chin. "There had to be something she ate no one else did," I insisted.

"Those stupid chocolates," Jez muttered.

I stared at her. "What?"

She flushed. "Um, the chocolates. Remember she was eating them last night? And the night before. That was the third box since she's been here. Or maybe it was the fourth. Anyway, she told me she gets them at Fortnum & Masons in London. She must spend a fortune on them."

"Did she finish that box last night?" I asked, trying to remember.

"Nope." Jez shook her head. "It was still about half full when she went to bed for the night. She took it up with her."

It hadn't been in her room. I'd looked. "We need to find that box."

"I'll check the bins in the kitchen," Bill offered.

"And I'll check the ones outside," said Rupert.

"Anywhere else they might have been tossed?" I asked.

Rupert gave me a helpless shrug. "One of the rooms, maybe? Or the hall bathroom."

"I'll check that," said Lucas.

The three men strode off purposefully on their missions. I kept my fingers crossed they would find something. Meanwhile, I was going to turn the drawing room upside down.

#

The fire in the drawing room had yet to be lit and the curtains hadn't been drawn yet. The entire room was cast into dark shadows. It was actually kind of creepy.

"Perfect place for a ghostly presence to appear, don't you think?" Jez's voice nearly had me jumping out of my skin. I turned to see her standing in the doorway, nervously clutching the frame with one hand. She wore a dark colored hoodie with a Star Wars logo on the left breast.

"What are you doing here?" I hissed.

"Wanted to see what you're up to," she said. "Figured you were onto something when you hustled out of the dining room. Bacon?" She held up a crispy strip in one hand.

"Uh, no thanks."

She shrugged. "Suit yourself." She munched on the bacon letting out a little moan of bliss. "When I first got here all they had was that weird stuff the British call bacon. I had to convince Rupert to buy the real deal. Fortunately he managed to get in a shopping trip right before the storm hit."

I tuned her out and focused on the drawing room. Marilyn had always sat in the armchair closest to the fire. And she'd always kept an open box of chocolates on the end table next to her. The only thing currently on the end table was a lamp, but that didn't mean the chocolate box wasn't nearby. I knelt down next to the chair and ran my hands between the cushion and the frame. Nothing. Not that I expected to find anything. Next, I lifted the chair and peered underneath. Still nothing.

Meanwhile, Jez was poking around under the couch. "Nothing here." Her voice was muffled since she was half-buried under the sofa cushions.

"Keep looking. It can't have just disappeared."

She sat back on her heels, frown line between her brows. "What if the killer burned them? The box and whatever chocolates were left. If there were any."

"Believe me, the thought had occurred. But I don't see anything in the fireplace down here." In fact, the thing had been swept clean. "I think we should talk to Anka. She's clearly been a busy bee."

"It's her job."

Still, suspicion rankled. "Let's finish searching this room and then we'll talk to Anka."

"You vant talk to me?" The strident voice boomed from behind us.

We spun around to find Anka standing in the doorway to the drawing room, hands propped on hips. She had a disgusted look on her face, making her look more sour than usual. Great, she'd overheard me all but accusing her of destroying evidence.

"Um, you cleaned the fireplace this morning, yes? Swept out the ash and whatnot?"

"Yes. That my job." She didn't soften one bit.

"Was there anything in it?" I asked.

She gave me a look that spoke volumes on her thoughts about my intelligence. "Vot you say. Ash."

"She means something *else*," Jez said helpfully. "Like someone tried to burn a box or something."

"No. Just ash. Some vood. Nothing more."

Curses. There went my theory.

"Okay, thanks, Anka." I offered her a conciliatory smile.

She snorted and muttered something in Polish. I don't think it was very nice.

The minute she was out of the room, Jez let out a giggle. "She's kind of scary. If I were writing a book, she'd definitely be the killer."

"Good thing you're not a novelist then," I said tartly. That just made her laugh harder. I wasn't sure why it was so funny. It was clear Anka wasn't involved. She had no motive that I could see. And the woman, though obviously strong, was unlikely to have dragged a dead body all over the house. Blodgett had been at least one hundred and eighty pounds. That dead weight would require some muscle to move. "Back to work," I said with false cheerfulness.

Fifteen minutes later we'd searched everywhere. Jez and I stood back by the fireplace and scanned the room.

"We looked everywhere. It's not here." She sounded disappointed.

My gaze lit on the side table next to Marilyn's chair. It was one of those tables that doubles as a small bookshelf and magazine rack with shelves along the front and a vee shaped holder in the back. The shelves were neatly filled with paperbacks and the holder was overflowing with magazines and newspapers. But there was a small space between the front feet just wide enough... I marched over to the side table and removed the lamp.

"What are you doing?" Jez asked.

"There's one place we haven't looked," I said and tilted the side table back just enough so I could peer underneath.

Beneath the table in a patch of dust sat a shiny, pink chocolate box. I smiled. "Gotcha."

Shéa MacLeod

Chapter 15
Poking a Bee Hive

I sent Jez to round up the Colonel and Lucas while I used tissue to cover my hands and remove the chocolate box. Hopefully I wouldn't mess up any fingerprints the killer might have left.

We met Lucas and Colonel Frampton in the kitchen. Bill was with them though Rupert had apparently shut himself in his office. I carefully placed the box in the middle of the butcher block. We all stared at it like it might bite.

"Bill," Lucas said, "do you happen to have a new pair of kitchen gloves on hand?"

"Better than that," Bill said. "I've got a box of surgical gloves. Use them for cutting up chilies." He strode to the sink and grabbed a pair of gloves from a box on the shelf above it.

I snagged the gloves from Bill before he could hand them over to Lucas. "I found the box. I want to be the one to open it."

The gloves were a little big, but they worked well enough. I lifted the lid from the box, careful to keep my fingers to the edges so as not to mess up fingerprints. Inside, about half a dozen uneaten chocolates lay nestled in their paper liners.

"They look fine," the colonel said, peering through a pair of half-moon reading glasses.

"Looks can be deceiving," I reminded him. I picked up one of the chocolates and held it to the light, carefully turning it over to examine every angle. "There." I pointed to the bottom of the chocolate.

"I don't see anything," the colonel insisted.

Jez rolled her eyes. "That's 'cuz you're old. I definitely see something. It's like a tiny little pin prick."

The colonel flushed crimson, though whether from anger or embarrassment it was hard to tell. "Well," he harrumphed.

"It's partially hidden by the hatch design on the bottom," Lucas said graciously. "Very difficult to see."

"But it's definitely there," I agreed. "I'm betting this is where the killer injected the chocolate with anti-freeze." I put the chocolate back and picked up another. Sure enough, there was another minute hole in the bottom. One at a time I examined each of the chocolates. "They've all got holes."

"Which means that likely all the chocolates in the box were injected with poison," Lucas said.

"Or at least half of them were," Jez interjected.

"What do you mean?" Lucas asked.

"I think this is Marilyn's second box from yesterday," Jez said. "Wednesday night she had half a box of chocolates left. It was a pale blue box. I saw her eating from it Thursday around lunch time. By dinner, she'd started in on a pink box." She pointed to the one sitting on the butcher block. "Had to be that one."

"All right, so she started on this box before dinner. I'm betting those weren't poisoned. Not based on when she died," I said. "Otherwise she would have been feeling sick at dinner."

"Definitely not," Jez said. "She was packing it away as usual. I've never seen anyone who could eat like Marilyn. Well, except this guy I dated a couple years ago. Frank. Skinny as a rail, but he could down two pizzas in a sitting. Large pizzas. Plus a six pack of beer. Made me homicidal. I gain weight if I even look at a pizza."

I totally felt her pain.

"All right," Lucas said, "whoever poisoned the remaining chocolates did it in the evening after Marilyn went to dinner. Did she take the chocolates with her?"

Jez shook her head. "I don't know. I was with Viola ghost hunting. But Marilyn always left them sitting on the lamp stand until she went up to bed."

"So, they had to have been poisoned while she was at dinner," Lucas said. "Who wasn't in the dining room when Marilyn was?" He glanced over at Colonel Frampton who shrugged.

"I'm afraid my memory isn't what it was, dear boy. Perhaps that's a question best put to the rest of the guests. Unless Bill knows?" He turned to Bill, one bushy eyebrow lifted.

"When I'm in the kitchen, I'm in my own world. I could tell you what was ordered, but not who ordered it."

"But you deliver the food, too," I pointed out.

He shrugged. "Yeah. Sometimes. And sometimes Rupert does."

"What about last night?" I prodded. "Jez and I weren't there, obviously. So, who was? Where did you deliver orders?"

He scrunched up his face in thought. "Shepherd's pie near the fire. That was the colonel. That girl with the flower name had a salad in her room." I could only assume he meant Lavender. "Shepherd's pie for Lucas at the bar. The professor had pie but her husband had fish and chips. They sat near the colonel. Fish and chips for the Carsleys, but they came in later. Service was almost through."

Which meant neither the Carsley's nor Lavender Wu had cast iron alibis for poisoning the chocolates. Problem was, none of them had motives that I could see.

"What I want to know is why the chocolates were under that table to begin with," Jez said. "She usually took them up to bed with her. She always joked about someone eating her expensive chocolates. I can't imagine her leaving them behind."

"I don't think she did leave them," I mused. "I'm betting she took them to bed with her as usual. After she was dead, the killer removed them when he, or she, left the syringe in order to confuse the issue."

"Then why didn't the killer just throw the box away? Or burn it?" Jez asked.

"Could be they planned to, but got waylaid. Maybe someone was up and about so they had to hide the box until later," I said.

"But we found it first!" She grinned. "We should be detectives."

Lucas groaned and Colonel Frampton looked horrified. As Bill shooed us out of the kitchen so he could begin lunch prep, I mulled over the three "suspects."

James had already been cleared of Blodgett's murder, so Marilyn claiming to know the identity of the killer wouldn't have bothered him. He knew he was innocent. I couldn't imagine Monica Carsley killing Blodgett and dragging his body around. Nor could I imagine her poisoning Marilyn. Lavender...I could definitely imagine her killing anyone who got in her way, but why Blodgett and Marilyn? Far as I could see, she had no reason. I'd just have to confront her and see what happened. I had a feeling it would be a little like poking a bee hive. But first, a little bit of online research.

# # #

I found Lavender curled up on the sofa in the drawing room, nose buried in a paperback novel. It had a lurid cover with a half-naked man—golden locks flowing in an imaginary breeze—and a woman half in and half out of her hoop skirts. It was very old-school bodice-ripper. Not at all what I imagined her reading, especially after her mockery earlier. Then again, after what I'd found online, nothing should surprise me.

I sat on the other end of couch and eyeballed her. At first she ignored me. Then she finally heaved a great sigh and put her book down. "What?" she snapped. Her tone was snide and her attitude superior. As usual.

"According to Bill, you didn't come down for dinner last night. You had salad in your room."

"So? Why is it any business of yours?" Her tone made it clear that it wasn't any of my business as far as she was concerned.

"Because it was during dinner that someone poisoned Marilyn Toppenish's chocolates, thus murdering her. You, Ms. Wu, do not have an alibi. Not for last night. And not for the morning of Jeffrey Blodgett's murder."

Her eyes grew hard. "Again, what business is it of yours? You're not the police."

"True," I admitted. "But the police have put Colonel Frampton in charge and he has requested my assistance." Which was sort of true. He would have asked if he'd realized how good I was at this sort of thing. "I would think an innocent person would want to make sure her name was cleared."

"I've got nothing to hide. I simply don't have an alibi. It wasn't like I expected two murders to happen."

I decided to go with my gut. "That's not true, is it?" I said. "That you don't have an alibi."

She gave me a blank look, but she fidgeted with the corner of the paperback cover, flicking it backward and forward between her fingers. "I don't know what you mean."

Aha! Now we were getting somewhere. "Let's start with last night. Where were you? Truth."

A muscle flexed in her jaw as she clearly warred with not wanting to tell me anything and wanting to make sure everyone knew she was innocent. "Fine," she snapped. "I was in my room, but I wasn't alone."

I lifted a brow, feigning shock. "Were you having a rendezvous with another guest?"

"Don't be crass. I was Skyping my girlfriend. She's currently in Norway on business and it was the only time I could speak to her. Satisfied?"

I shrugged. "That can be easily checked."

"Go right ahead." She raised her book. "Now, if you don't mind, I'm busy."

"Actually, I do mind." I eyed her closely. "I'm curious to know if your girlfriend is aware you've been having an affair with Martin Huxton-Barrington."

"What?" she shrieked. She glanced around as if to ensure the professor wasn't lurking anywhere. Lowering her voice she demanded, "How did you find out?"

"A little bird told me." Actually, it had been a quick search through social media. Lavender wasn't exactly a rocket scientist when it came to keeping her affair a secret. She'd posted a selfie of her and Martin on her Facebook page for the world to see. She'd even tagged him. Granted, she'd declared him her "good friend," but body language is telling. As is a trip to the south of France. Add that to the fact the two of them had pretended they didn't know each other and it added up to an affair.

"Fine," she said, tossing the book on the coffee table. It landed with a thud and skidded off the smooth glass onto the floor. "You're obviously not going to let this go, but you need to swear to me this doesn't leave the room."

"I swear." She didn't need to know I kept my fingers crossed behind my back.

"Martin and I have been having an affair for over a year now."

"What about your girlfriend?" I asked, curious more than anything.

Lavender shrugged. "She knows. We have an open relationship."

I was never sure how people managed that. If I caught Lucas sleeping around, I'd flay him alive. But, hey, whatever works. "So, your girlfriend knew, but I take it Professor Huxton-Barrington doesn't?"

"Abigail? Don't be daft. She'd kill us both. Then divorce Martin and leave him with nothing. They're reasonably well off, but all the money is hers, you see." She shook her head, her silken hair sliding around her shoulders like a shampoo model. "Anyway, we've had to be really careful, but it's been getting harder and harder what with the professor going into semi-retirement and being home a lot more now. And then this trip..." She made a moue of disgust. "This week is the anniversary of the day we met. Martin and I were supposed to spend it together while Abigail was at some symposium in York, but she cancelled at the last minute and insisted they come to this dump in the middle of nowhere."

"Pretty nice dump." Things were clicking into place.

"Whatever." She scowled at the drawing room as if she found the elegant yet cozy furnishings a personal affront to good taste. She probably lived in a high-rise flat in London with ultra-modern furniture and everything white.

"I'm guessing the car accident wasn't really an accident."

She snorted. "Give the woman a gold star. No, it wasn't. I figured if I showed up a victim of a car accident, Abigail would never guess I was really there to see Martin. So, I drove up the day after they arrived. My plan was to just drive the car off the road and get it stuck in a ditch or whatnot, but the rain spoiled that plan and I crashed instead. Still, it all worked out in the end."

I was sure the car insurance company would be thrilled with her assessment. "And when Jeffrey Blodgett was killed, you were in bed with Martin."

"Of course. I don't know why that idiot Rupert claimed to have seen Martin in the garden. We were together in my room from twenty minutes past nine, when his wife left their room, until everyone started screaming."

"And his wife never suspected a thing?"

Lavender rolled her eyes. "For being such a smart person, the professor is a world class imbecile."

Shéa MacLeod

Chapter 16
The Secret Passage

"Of course I knew about Martin's little floozy." Professor Huxton-Barrington gave me a thin smile. Her pale blue mock-turtle neck was particularly unflattering to her skin tone, and she wore yet another tweed skirt. "It's been going on for months, now."

I'd found Abigail Huxton-Barrington in the bar sitting next to the fire with her tablet. Rupert had decided to keep the bar open all day since the library was off limits. I pulled over another armchair and took a seat.

"And you're not upset about the affair?" I asked, surprised at her calm.

"At first I was," she admitted, laying her tablet on the table. I'm pretty good at reading upside down and it looked like one of those tacky articles on face exercises that made you look younger. My mother was into those. I wasn't sure they worked. Plus the professor didn't look like she needed them. Her neck and cheeks seemed unusually taught for a woman approaching sixty. "But then I realized that his shagging her kept him out of my bed. And, as far as I'm concerned, the farther from my bed he is, the better. I can see you're quite shocked."

"Er, quite." I couldn't help myself. "I can't imagine too many wives would be quite so pragmatic about wandering husbands."

"That's because you are American." She folded her hands primly in her lap. It was her hands that betrayed her age. The skin was thin and crêpe-y with prominent veins and several age spots. "I'm very well aware that Martin married me for my money and position. He's always been easily impressed by those things."

Talk about the pot calling the kettle black. The woman was obsessed with propriety and appearances. "Sounds like you don't like him much."

"Not really. He was useful once. It's always nice to have a handsome man on your arm at soirees. Impresses the hierarchy. But now I find him tedious."

I blinked. "So, why don't you just divorce him?"

Her eyes widened behind the thick lenses of her tortoiseshell glasses. "But that would never do. I have an image to maintain. Can you imagine how the Oxford Council would view such a distasteful display of poor manners?"

"I'm not sure divorce is considered poor manners." At least not in the last several decades.

"It's simply not done. Perhaps when I retire fully, but until then I am afraid we are stuck together. He will find it very difficult to divorce me." She actually smirked. I was starting the think the woman might be slightly unhinged.

"Let me get this straight, you knew that Martin and Lavender were, uh…"

"In bed together," she said placidly.

"Yes. That. You knew they were in bed together during the time of the first murder?"

"Indeed. Frankly, I was relieved to get away from his whining for a bit. I had work to do," she said primly.

"Right. Studying that particular first edition book. Which one was it?"

"Pardon?"

I turned to her, a slight smile quirking my lips. "Which book were you studying? I'd love to look at it."

"Um, I put it back in the wrong place, so I'm afraid I'm not sure." Her smile made her face look like a plastic doll. I wondered vaguely how much surgery she'd had, and if losing her man to a younger woman really had been fine with her.

"Sure. Okay. If you insist." I stood up.

"I do." Her voice dripped with ice.

I'd a feeling I'd get no more from the professor. Still, I'd a pretty good idea where I could get more information, so I gave her a little wave—which she ignored—and slipped out of the room. I wanted to track down Anka. I had a feeling about the housekeeper and, if I was right, she'd be able to help me with the professor.

I found her in the utility closet on the first floor sorting through extra towels. Her hair was up in its usual severe bun, and her lips were pursed as if sucking on a lemon.

"Hey, Anka."

She slid me a sideways glance. "Vat you vant? I'm busy."

"Yeah, I see that. You're very good at your job. Our room is always nice and clean and I love that you put out fresh towels every day."

She softened visibly. "I take pride in vork."

"As you should." I stepped closer and lowered my voice. "Listen, Anka, when you're cleaning rooms I know you're really busy, but I'm sure you can't help noticing a thing or two."

Her expression hardened again. "I not a snoop."

"Never said you were. I'm just staying, a smart woman like you? You might have seen something. A clue, perhaps."

Her eyes widened. "A clue? Like on Poirot?" She pronounced the "t" on the end of the name.

"Oh, yes," I breathed as if it were the most exciting thing in the world. I had her now. She was one of my people. "You might not even have realized you saw something. You see, detectives, they rely on intelligent people like you to help them solve cases. Is there anything? Anything at all?"

I could see the gears whirling in her head. She didn't want to admit to snooping and get fired. On the other hand, she was used to being ignored, so the opportunity to be the center of attention and do something important was alluring.

"Don't worry," I assured her. "You won't get in trouble. You can't help it if you see something while cleaning, now, can you?"

"No. You are right." She gave a snappy nod. "I tell you. Vot you vant to know?"

"Whatever you can tell me."

She gave me a sly look. "That Professor, her husband iz sleeping with that nasty woman. The vone vit the black hair."

"Lavender Wu?"

"Yes. I see him coming out her room. Then I find his pants in sheets and used condom in rubbish."

I knew by "pants" she meant underwear. That's what the British called them.

"Very interesting." I didn't bother to tell her I already knew that. "What else?"

"The colonel? He vas vatching dirty movies."

"Really? When?" Oh, Colonel Frampton, you naughty man.

"Alla time."

"What about the day Jeffrey Blodgett was killed?" The colonel had no alibi before ten twenty-five when he joined the professor for a drink.

Anka scrunched up her face in thought. "Ya. He left telly on. Vas quite a surprise, you know vot I mean?" She waggled her thick, dark eyebrows. I desperately wanted to take a tweezer to them. Instead, I forced myself to focus.

"Yep, I get it. What about the professor? Anything interesting in her room? Clue-wise, I mean."

"Not that day, but the next, ya."

"What?" I was on pins and needles.

"She have a book from the manor library in her room."

"Oh," I said, disappointed. "She's been studying one. Some first edition."

"No. You not understand. It vos not on desk, it vos in..." she flushed as if suddenly realizing her admission would give her away.

"Please, Anka. I swear, I won't tell anybody you're the one that told me."

She leaned forward and whispered. "It vos in her luggage."

# # #

"So, the professor was trying to steal a first edition book?" Jez asked. I'd run into her in the hallway and dragged her into my room. I'd given her the rundown on Lavender, Martin, and the colonel, as well as the professor and her little theft.

"You don't seem surprised," I said.

She chewed her lower lip. "Well, I'm not really. See, they arrived the night after I did. I was headed into dinner while they were checking in and I think they have money problems."

"Why do you say that?"

"Well, like with most hotels, Rupert doesn't charge until you check out, right? But he does hold a night's stay on your credit card in case you damage something."

"Okay. A lot of hotels do that," I said.

She nodded. "Exactly. But the professor threw a fit over it. Her credit card was declined and she had to give him another one. She was quite snippy about the whole thing."

"So, if money is tight, why has she gone semi-retired? Unless she was forced to."

"Could be," Jez agreed. "That's not uncommon. Reach a certain age and they try to toss you to the wolves."

"Maybe she's older than I realized."

"She's nearly seventy. Martin's like fifteen years younger than she is."

That surprised me. "She must have an excellent plastic surgeon."

"Hollywood," Jez said with utter confidence.

"That would cost a pretty penny. No wonder she's short on cash. It would explain her stealing that book."

"We should look it up." Jez pulled out her smart phone. "What's the title?"

"*An Essay Concerning Humane Understanding* by John Locke. Wow. 1690. That's old."

"I've heard of him." Jez tapped at her phone screen. "Holy bananas. A similar book sold at Sotheby's last year."

Sotheby's was an auction house for the rich and exotic. "What did it sell for?" I asked.

"Over sixteen thousand."

"Dollars?"

She grinned. "Nope. Pounds."

Which, depending on the exchange rate, was twenty to twenty-five thousand dollars. "That would pay for some Botox."

Jez tucked her phone back in her pocket. "You think that's what the professor has been doing? Visiting manor houses and stealing valuable books? And for what? So she can look like Joan Rivers, God rest her soul."

"Seems that way. Maybe she's more upset by Martin's philandering than she'd have us believe." It was sad, really. An aging woman so desperate to hang on to her younger husband she was willing to do anything to regain her lost youth. I felt kind of sorry for Professor Huxton-Barrington.

"She'd be better off with a dog," Jez said tartly. "At least they're loyal."

"The professor doesn't strike me as a dog person," I said. She wasn't much of a people person, for that matter.

"In other news. I found something interesting." Jez's eyes lit up.

"You finally get your ghost?"

"Unfortunately, not, but this is cool. Come on."

I followed her downstairs. She made a right turn in the lobby. The door to Rupert's office was closed, but she pushed it open. I expected to find Rupert seated at his desk, annoyed at being interrupted, but the room was empty.

"I was in here early this morning taking some readings when I noticed a bit of a draft," Jez said, tripping across the thick, Persian rug that took up most of the floor space.

"Maybe the windows leak. It's an old building," I suggested. "Or the flue in the fireplace could be open."

She shook her head, a cheeky grin splitting her face. "Nope. It was coming from over here." She patted the row of floor to ceiling bookshelves that had been built into one wall of the office. There were three of them about eight feet tall and four feet wide. On either side of the shelves were a pair of sconces with milky, globe shaped glass. "Check it out."

Curious, I joined her at the bookshelves. "I can't feel anything."

"Trust me, it's there."

I licked my finger and held it up to the joint between two of the shelves. Sure enough, I could feel a faint, chill breeze coming from between the shelves. "Crimeny! You're right."

Her smile grew smug. "Watch this." She reached up, grabbed one of the sconces, and gave it a twist. The middle shelf popped open about an inch or two. The hinges made a loud squeal as Jez grabbed the edge and swung it open. "Welcome to Wytham Manor's secret passage."

Shéa MacLeod

Chapter 17
Exploratory Mission

"Have you explored it yet?" I asked, peering into the secret passage, my heart thudding with excitement.

"A little," Jez said.

There was just enough light to see that what lay beyond the bookshelves was a narrow passage leading downward. The pool of light illuminated the top of what appeared to be a staircase that turned to the right. Jez pulled out her phone and switched on its flashlight. As she shone it around, I could see the bare brick and timber walls and unfinished plank floors. Jez had made footprints in the thick dust on the steps, but otherwise it looked like it hadn't been disturbed in decades. Heavy cobwebs draped the corners and I shuddered thinking of how many spiders must be running around in there.

It was my first secret passage and excitement shimmered inside me like champagne bubbles. I wanted those stairs to lead to a hidden treasure room. Or out to a beach where pirates smuggled their loot. Not that we were anywhere near a beach.

"I went as far as the bottom of the stairs, but..." she trailed off, a slight blush staining her pale cheeks, partially obscuring her freckles.

"But what?"

"I was nervous," she admitted. "It's silly, me being a ghost hunter and all, but I started thinking, what if I got locked in or something? My cell phone doesn't work inside the passage. The walls are too thick. No one would know I was in here."

"That's smart, actually. At least if I'm with you, you won't die alone."

"Thanks. That's encouraging," she said drily.

I followed her through the narrow, cobwebby doorway and onto the stairs. The walls were so close, I kept snagging the sleeves of my cobalt blue sweater on the rough bricks. Our feet sent up little poufs of dust with each step and the treads creaked ominously beneath our weight.

At the end of the stairwell, the passage stretched straight on before ending in another set of steps, this time going up.

At the top of the stairs there was a short turn to the right before the hall dead ended into a wall covered in peeling, floral wallpaper. We both stared at it.

"Well, bugger," Jez said. "I was hoping there'd be another door or something."

I frowned. "The other walls are brick."

"So?"

"So, why's this one covered in flowers? I'm betting *this* is the door."

Jez's eyes lit up. "I can't believe I didn't think of that."

We spent several minutes poking and prodding and pushing on the wall to no avail. I finally took a break. "There's got to be an easier way." A thought occurred. "I know, why don't we figure out where the passage comes out? Maybe we can open it from the other side."

"Good idea!" Jez grinned. "How do we do that?"

"By following it from up top," I said. "You okay if I leave you for a minute?"

She didn't look okay, but she swallowed and said, "Sure." For a ghost hunter, she was kind of a scaredy cat.

I hurried back the way we'd come, counting each step to make sure I could duplicate my movements. I let myself into Rupert's office. It was still empty and I wondered where he was. I wanted to question him about his lack of alibi and lying about seeing Martin, but right now I'd other fish to fry.

On the other side of the shelves, I paused, trying to visualize the passage we'd taken. The stairs had led to the right. So, I trailed along the bookcase to the right which led me...to the door of Rupert's office. I stopped. The passage had continued straight ahead, which would take me into the lobby. With a shrugged I crossed the lobby, counting my steps as I had on the trip back. They brought me to within a couple feet of a wall. I frowned. What was on the other side of that wall?

I turned right, just as the passage had, before stumbling to a halt. There was only one room that the passage could possibly lead to. Holy fish sticks.

# # #

Jez blinked as I swung open the secret passage. "Took you long enough. What—." And then she stopped as she realized where she stood. She gazed around in wonder as she stepped out of the passage. "But this is the library."

I grinned. "Exactly."

Once I'd figured it out, things had become very clear. And it had been easy enough to find the passage on the other side. The matching sconces were a dead giveaway, pardon the pun.

"Have a look in the passage," I suggested. "What do you see?"

She turned to look. "I don't know. Same as the other side, I guess. Brick walls and whatnot."

"Maybe I should ask, what *don't* you see?"

She frowned. "I'm sorry, I don't get it."

"Dust! The entire passageway is covered in dust except for this landing." I stepped in and shone my phone's flashlight on the floor. "See. It's like something heavy was dragged through the dust leaving a clean spot."

Jez's eyes widened. "You mean…? Wait, what *do* you mean?"

"I've had my suspicions, but now I'm sure. Whoever strangled Jeffrey Blodgett didn't want his body found right away. So, they dragged him in here after killing him. Later, they pulled him back out and propped him in that chair so he could be found. When James Carsley found him, he thought Blodgett was still alive and stabbed him with the letter opener."

"That's crazy. But it makes sense. How do we figure out who did it?"

"Obviously it had to be someone who knew the house well enough to know there's a secret passage," I said.

"The only ones I know would be Rupert and Bill. They run the place, after all. Everyone else is just a visitor and that passage hasn't been used in years." Jez frowned. "I mean, somebody could have stumbled on it like I did."

I thought about that, but it felt wrong. "Unlikely. I'm guessing they knew it was here. The murder may have been spur of the moment—manual strangulations usually are impulsive—but the killer would have had to hide the body fast. There were literally only a few moments between James leaving the library and the professor arriving. There would have been no time to accidentally stumble on a secret hiding place."

"So, who do we start with first?" Jez asked. "Rupert or Bill?"

"What are you ladies doing in here?"

We both whirled to find Rupert himself standing in the doorway to the library exuding as much indignation as his rolly poly frame could muster. He looked like an angry elf.

"Rupert. Just the man I wanted to see." I gave him my most charming smile, hoping to distract him from the fact we'd entered a crime scene.

He drew himself up to his full five foot two. "You're not supposed to be in here. I must report this to the colonel immediately."

Okay, so charm wasn't going to work. I went on the offensive. "You go right ahead, Rupert. And while you're at it, you can explain to him why you murdered Jeffrey Blodgett."

"What?" He backed away from me as if I'd gone rabid, his face sweaty and pale. "I did no such thing! I never met the man until he checked in here. Why would I kill him?"

"Who else could it be?" I asked, stalking toward him with my scariest expression firmly in place. I'd perfected it years ago when working with difficult clients who refused to listen to me when it came to their accounting. "After Blodgett was murdered, someone stuffed him in the secret passage."

"What secret passage?" Rupert whimpered.

"That secret passage," Jez said, pointing behind us to the bookshelf that stood open.

"You had to have known it was here," I continued. "Who else but the manager of the inn would know about a secret passage?"

"B-but I didn't. I swear, I had no idea." Rupert was literally shaking now. "No one ever told me."

"But you could have stumbled on it while exploring the place," Jez said matter-of-factly.

"I'm not exactly the exploring type," he pointed out.

Which, from what I'd seen of Rupert, was absolutely true. Besides which, I couldn't imagine short, round Rupert hauling the much taller and heavier Blodgett into the narrow landing. It just didn't compute. And, like he said, what would be his motive? I decided to take another tack.

"Okay, so if you didn't kill Blodgett and stuff him in the stairwell, why did you lie?"

Rupert swallowed, his Adam's apple bobbing wildly. "Um, what do you mean?"

I smiled grimly. "You claimed you were in your office at the time of Blodgett's death and that you'd seen Martin wandering around in the garden."

"It's true. I was in my office."

"But it's not true," Jez said.

"I don't know what you mean," Rupert wailed.

"You couldn't have seen Martin in the garden because Martin was in bed with Lavender Wu," Jez said triumphantly.

"Clearly you lied about seeing Martin," I said. "Did you lie about being in your office? Maybe you were in the library killing Blodgett."

"No! No! I was in my office like I said, I was just..." he trailed off.

"You better spill it," I snapped. "Because from where I stand, your lies only make you look guilty. Why would you lie about seeing Martin?"

"Because I need an alibi," Rupert wailed. "I didn't have one and when Martin said he was in the garden, I figured I was safe. I'd just say I saw him."

"Where were you really?" I demanded.

He seemed to shrink in on himself. "You can't tell Bill, okay?"

I frowned. "Why not?"

"Because I promised I'd stop."

Jez and I exchanged glances. I couldn't imagine what awful thing he could have been doing that he needed to lie about it. "What? Were you watching porn or something?"

"No. Nothing like that." He sank into a chair by the library door. "I used to have a drinking problem, you see. In fact, Bill and I broke up over it for a while. When we got back together, I promised I'd quit for good. And I had. But then there was the storm, and stress..." he sighed and laid his head back on the chair. "It was more than I could handle. I figured one sip now and then wouldn't hurt. So, I keep a bottle locked in my desk drawer. And that's what I was doing when Blodgett was killed."

It was my turn to sink into a chair. He'd been drinking in secret and he'd only lied so his boyfriend didn't find out and dump him again. I let out a groan of frustration. There went my main suspect.

Chapter 18
Spirits of the Dead

"Let's do a séance."

Lucas, Colonel Frampton, and I stared at Jez like she'd just sprouted a second head. A green one. With tentacles.

We were all having lunch in the hotel bar. Bill had whipped up sandwiches and scones. Over the meal, Jez and I had given Lucas and the colonel a run-down on our latest discovery. The colonel had not been pleased about our invasion of the crime scene, but the discovery of the secret passage had piqued his interest.

"We can get everyone together," Jez continued. "See if we can contact Blodgett and Marilyn. Ask them who killed them. I mean, don't you think that would be interesting? And since they were killed here, the experts claim their spirits should still linger."

"My dear girl," the colonel said, patting his moustache with a napkin, "we are in the midst of a murder investigation. We do not need to waste our time in such trivial pursuits."

"I disagree," I said.

"Of course you would," he said with a patronizing air which set my hackles on end.

Lucas laid his hand on my leg, trying to prevent the eruption building inside me. Apparently, clenching my fists is a sign of bad things to come.

"I agree with Viola," he said, giving me a sideways glance that begged me to shut up. "It will get everyone's minds off things. And, if we do it right..."

The colonel leaned forward. "Yes?"

Lucas grinned. "We might catch ourselves a killer."

The colonel tugged at his moustache. "Intriguing. Do go on."

"Over to you, Jez," Lucas said graciously.

"Well, it's easy enough, I guess. We do the usual thing. Get everyone around the table and ask the ghosts of the murder victims to put in an appearance. If they don't come..."

I rolled my eyes.

"...then I can step in," Jez continued as if she hadn't seen me. "Pretend to channel Marilyn's ghost, for instance. Say that I know who the killer is and so on."

"And that will hopefully flush him or her out," I said.

We discussed the various technical aspects of the séance, such as location, candles vs. lamps, and whether or not there should be music. Once we set a time, we all scattered to issue invitations to the other guests and to rope Bill and Rupert into helping us set up. Jez grabbed my arm as I got up from the table.

"Here's the thing," Jez said, glancing around to make sure the men were out of ear shot. "I've never actually done a séance before."

I stared at her. "Are you kidding me? This was your suggestion."

"Yes, I know. I've seen them done, of course. My mom does it all the time. She used to do them in our house when I was a kid, but now she lives in a studio, she does them in the shop. They're hugely popular. I swear she makes more money from séances than she does selling coffee. And you know how we West Coast people love our coffee."

It was true. As a native Oregonian, my blood was a pretty even mix of rainwater and caffeine. My mother insisted I drank too much of the stuff. She'd quit years ago and now only drank herbal tea. She said she felt so much better and had more energy. I wasn't sure how that was even possible. Besides which, I didn't just drink it for myself. I drank it for the safety of others. Talking to me before my first cup in the morning was a very dangerous thing.

"Okay, so you've seen your mom do it. Think you can replicate it, at least?"

"I think so," she said. "At least well enough to fool people. For the most part, it's theatrics. Although in my mom's case, she's the real deal."

Was she serious? "Excuse me?"

"Mom's a sensitive. I mean, I told you ghosts aren't like what we see in the movies. They're more like...impressions people leave behind. She can pick up on those old emotions and whatnot. She can feel what they felt in life. And that's what she passes on to her clients."

"A sensitive." I knew I was repeating things, but I couldn't help it.

"Unfortunately, I didn't get her gift. I guess that's why I started ghost hunting. I want to prove to all the people who've made fun of her and people like her that the ghosts are real. Maybe I can't see or feel them like she can, but I know they're real."

I shook my head. "Fine. Whatever. As long as you can do this thing convincingly. It's the best chance we have of forcing the killer's hand."

She frowned. "Is it safe?"

"Are you kidding? Lucas was in the Israeli army. If anyone can keep you safe, he can." I might still be pissed at him, but I had no questions about his abilities.

"Okay." She didn't look totally convinced, but she wandered off to collect whatever accoutrements she needed for her little theatrical event. At least it would get me out of another night of ghost hunting.

#

At around eleven-thirty that night, I made my way into the drawing room where Rupert and Bill had set up a round table large enough to seat everyone. The table was draped with a cream-colored lace cloth. A single candlestick with a white wax taper candle sat in the middle of the table. I assumed it was for focus or something. Near it was a box of matches. Jez stood next to the table fiddling with something.

I stared at her. "What are you doing? And what on earth are you wearing?"

She had a turban on her head made from what looked like old curtain material. The large floral pattern was very 70s, as was the odd polyester sheen. She wore a black and white silk kimono over jeans and a *Doctor Who* t-shirt.

"It's ridiculous, isn't it? But Bill insisted I look the part." She lifted the hem of the kimono with a frown. "This is his robe, apparently. I hope he washed it."

Gross. "Right, but that doesn't answer the question: what are you doing?"

"Oh, this is part of my equipment. I'm going to record the session. Both video and audio. I can check it later to see if we got any visitors." Her eyes sparkled with excitement.

I was at a loss for words. This was all fake. Something to goad the killer. She was acting like she thought an actual ghost might show up and parade around in front of the camera. I pinched the bridge of my nose and begged anyone listening to give me patience.

"All righty, then," I said with false cheer. "Let's get this show on the road. What should I do?"

"Nothing we can do but wait for the others to join us. Okay, I think that's good." She gave a last adjustment to her equipment and then plopped down in one of the chairs at the table. "When everyone's here, we'll light the candle and dim the overhead lights. Then we can begin. I hope they're all into this."

"Sure," I muttered. I didn't give a toss if anyone was "into" it or not. I just wanted to goad the killer into revealing himself. Or herself. I hadn't ruled out a woman as the killer, though it seemed less likely since whoever killed Blodgett had dragged his body into the secret passage and then back to the desk chair. That would have taken a lot of strength. I mean, just about anyone could heave him out of the chair and drag him across the floor, but getting him *back* was another story. I wasn't even sure I could do it, never mind tiny Monica Carsley or slender Lavender Wu. The professor was a tall, spare woman who *might* have the strength to pull it off. She certainly had strength of character.

The rest of the guests began to filter in, urged on by Lucas and the colonel. Not everyone had been thrilled with the idea.

"This is ridiculous," the professor complained loudly, as if to prove my point. "Séances are for the weak minded."

"Just shut up and sit down, will you, Abigail?" Martin said shortly.

"Shut up, you disgusting man," she snapped.

"Trouble in paradise," Lucas muttered as he sat down beside me. I was sitting across from Jez so I could keep an eye on things. Just in case.

"I don't think that particular marriage could ever have been described as paradise," I whispered back. "When I talked to her, I got the feeling she never liked him much."

"Then why did she marry him?"

"Don't ask me," I said. "People are weird." I eyed him meaningfully.

He sighed. "Viola…"

"Now is not the time."

Lavender Wu sat down on Lucas's other side with a smug smile aimed in my direction. I didn't get her deal.

She was supposedly having a hot and heavy affair with Martin, yet she took the opportunity to flirt with Lucas and throw it in my face every chance she got. If she thought she'd upset me, she was barking up the wrong tree. If I've learned one thing in my life it's this: You can't force people to love you or want to be with you, nor can you take anyone away who doesn't want to be taken. Lucas was with me. Period. Worrying about things that might happen was a waste of time and energy.

Granted, I'd spent a lot of time resisting any sort of commitment, but I'd gotten over that. Mostly. Besides, that had been more about me and my past than any worry about Lucas.

Martin made as if to sit on Lavender's other side, but the colonel beat him to it. I wasn't sure if it was on purpose or not. Martin was forced to sit in between his wife, who was on Jez's left, and the colonel. Neither of the Huxton-Barrigtons looked thrilled to be sitting next to each other.

On Jez's right was Monica Carsley. Oddly enough, James didn't sit next to Monica. Instead he sat two chairs down with Anka, the maid, between them. She was muttering something in Polish while fingering the gold cross around her neck. Next to her was Bill with Rupert tucked between him and me.

"Good, we're all here," Jez said. "We can begin." She lit the candle in front of her. "Rupert, can you dim the lights, please?"

Rupert walked to the fireplace, took a remote control off the mantle, and pointed it at the chandelier. The bulbs dimmed and the room was cast into long shadows. The single candle glowed cheerfully as Rupert replaced the remote on the mantle and took his seat. Jez gave us all a stern look.

"Now, we are about to touch the spirit world. It's very important that you follow my instructions to the letter."

The professor muttered something about idiots and small minds. Lavender rolled her eyes. Anka prayed harder. The rest of us nodded our agreement.

"Good. I need everyone to hold hands and don't let go until the séance is over no matter what happens."

We all grabbed hands. Rupert's was a bit sweaty. Lucas's was firm, and warm. He ran a thumb across my inner wrist which made me shiver. Naughty man. Did he not know I was still mad at him?

Jez raised her voiced in a sing song intonation. "We ask for protection as we enter the spirit realm." She swayed back and forth a little. "A circle of protection be around us." She took Monica and Martin's hands and closed her eyes. "The circle is complete. Spirits, are you listening? Is anyone there? Please, give us a sign."

The room was still as we all stared at each other. It was more than a little awkward. Anka was rocking back and forth muttering in Polish. A prayer, probably. Lavender was smirking at me. The professor gave a less than quiet huff.

"Please," Jez intoned. "Rap once if you can hear me."

There was a pause, and then a very distinct rap. We all nearly jumped out of our seats. Anka looked like she might faint. The professor's mouth dropped open in shock, and the knock wiped the smirk right off Lavender's face. My turn to smirk. I knew very well it was Lucas.

"Spirit, thank you for coming," Jez said. "Please identify yourself. Are you Jeffrey Blodgett?"

Silence.

"Marilyn Toppenish?"

A single, loud knock. I tried to figure out where it was coming from, but it was hard to tell. Lucas had been very clever.

"Marilyn, welcome. Do you know who killed you? One knock for yes, two for no."

There was a pause and it seemed everyone held their breath. Then came one knock. Anka let out a squeal of terror.

"Marilyn, we need you to tell us who killed you so that he or she can be brought to justice." Jez sucked in a deep breath. "Please use me as your vessel to communicate to us the identity of your murderer."

Her head fell back, then lifted slowly up. Her eyes opened, and she stared glassily at us. A smile curved her full lips and it chilled me to the bone. She was either a very good actress or... I couldn't believe the "or" was possible.

"Hello, everyone." The voice that came from Jez's mouth wasn't hers. It was garbled, altered, filled with amused superiority. "So nice of you to visit."

"Marilyn, is that you?" the Colonel asked. The tips of his moustache trembled.

"Hey, hot stuff. It's me." She literally waggled her eyebrows. It was creepy as all get out.

"Marilyn, who killed you?" he asked.

Her gaze roved the table, that superior smile growing wider. "It was—."

The lights went out, plunging the room into near darkness. Smoke wafted across the table as a sudden breeze doused the candles. I could hardly see my hand in front of my face. Somebody screamed. There was a thud, then the clatter of a chair falling over.

"Somebody get the lights." Lucas shouted.

"I can't see!" Monica cried.

"*Boże pomóż nam.*" I was guessing that was Anka praying in Polish.

"Shut up, everyone!" Pretty sure the nasty snarl came from James Carsley.

The lights finally came back on. The first thing I saw was Jez slumped across the table, blood pouring from a wound on the back of her head.

Chapter 19
Once Upon a Midnight Dreary

"Follow my finger." Lucas held his finger up in front of Jez's face and waved it back and forth.

"I'm fine, guys, really." She winced as Bill pressed a wet cloth to her scalp.

"It looks superficial," he said. "You know how head wounds are. A shallow cut can make you bleed like a stuck pig."

"Don't be so crass," Rupert snapped. He was looking a little green around the gills.

"Doesn't look like you have a concussion." Lucas stepped back. "But to be on the safe side, you should get plenty of rest. Take something for the pain and go to sleep."

"My dear boy, everyone knows you should stay awake if you have a concussion," the colonel said.

Lucas gave him a small smile. "I'm afraid that's a myth, sir. Doctors now recommend sleep to heal the brain as long as the injured is able to communicate fully and isn't staggering around or anything."

While they argued I sat down next to Jez and handed her an icepack. "I'm so sorry."

"It's not your fault," she said.

"Still, I'm going to figure out who did it. That séance was pretty convincing, by the way."

She smiled a little. "It was, wasn't it?"

"So, it *was* fake."

Her smile widened. "My lips are sealed."

I glared at her. "Well, as long as you're okay."

"I'm fine," Jez repeated, heaving herself off the chair in the kitchen where Bill had been tending her. She winced a little. "Although I've definitely got a headache. A pain killer and sleep sound really good." She glanced over at me. "Did you get what you needed?"

I frowned. "Maybe. I'll have to give it some thought."

She sighed. "I was hoping we'd get a confession or something."

The colonel chuckled. "My dear girl, this isn't the movies."

We all ignored him. His superior attitude was more than a little annoying.

"I'll bring you some tea," Rupert offered.

"Thanks, but I'll pass," Jez said. "I just want to crawl in bed."

"I'll help you up the stairs," Bill offered. "I know. You're fine. But just in case."

"You okay?" I asked Rupert as Bill and Jez exited the kitchen. "You seem a little...stressed."

"Bill's been on my case about the drinking," he muttered. "It's so irritating. Especially since I know he wasn't exactly behaving himself."

"What do you mean?"

"Did you ever wonder what Bill was doing the day Blodgett was killed?"

I thought about it. "Well, he said Anka was helping him from about ten until the body was found."

"But before that, he has no alibi. Do you know why?"

"Um, no," I admitted.

"He was outside. *Smoking*." Rupert said it like you'd say he was murdering someone.

"How do you know?" I asked. "I thought you were getting drunk in your office."

"I was. But after he gave me grief for that and threatened to leave me, I pointed out he had no alibi and maybe he'd been off killing Blodgett. He finally admitted he was taking a smoke break out back."

"And this is a problem because…" I prompted.

"Because he promised me he quit. He lied! And after giving me grief about drinking, too." He crossed his arms and thrust out his lower lip. He looked like a pouting elf. I tried really hard not to laugh.

"Rupert, one other question. Is there another remote to the drawing room chandelier other than the one you used?"

"No. That's the only one."

"Is there any other way to control the lights besides the remote and the switch?" I asked.

His brow furrowed. "Well, technically they can be controlled by a smartphone, but you'd have to download the app and know our password."

"Who knows the password?"

"Just myself and Bill. Neither of us brought our phones to the séance, though. Jez asked everyone not to. I locked mine in my desk drawer."

"You're sure Bill didn't have his?" I asked.

"Positive. I watched him set it on the counter in the kitchen. It was still here when we brought Jez in."

"So, someone would have had to hack your password in order to turn out the lights?"

"I don't see how else they could have done it," Rupert agreed.

"Well," said the colonel turning back from bidding Jez goodnight. "I'm not certain that accomplished anything except for an evening of amusement and a cleaning bill for the table cloth. Not to mention the injury to poor Ms. Montgomery's head. Who do you suppose did it?"

"Could have been Martin," Lucas said. "He was sitting beside her. Easy enough to bash her when the lights went out."

"But why?" I asked. "He's in the clear for Blodgett's murder which means he had no reason to kill Marilyn and therefore no reason to hit Jez."

"Maybe he was protecting someone?" Rupert suggested.

It was possible, but it felt all wrong. I turned to Lucas. "By the way, how'd you rig the knocking sound? It was perfect."

"I didn't. I mean, I rigged up something, but I never used it," Lucas admitted.

Rupert's eyes widened. "There really was a ghost."

"More likely someone very human was knocking," Lucas said dryly. "Question is, who and why?"

I rubbed my forehead. A headache was blossoming behind my eyes. "I'm tired. I need some sleep. Maybe things will be clearer in the morning."

But I couldn't sleep. I lay awake, staring at the canopy that loomed above like a ghostly presence. Lucas snored softly beside me. The man could sleep anywhere, anytime. Drat him.

I decided to go over the scene again. I pictured each person as they sat around the table. We'd all been in our places when the lights had gone out. What had happened at that moment?

I scrunched my eyes closed, trying to picture it. Yes. We'd all turned and stared at the chandelier. Like anyone would do. Even me. And at that precise moment, when we'd all been staring at the chandelier, there was that breeze and the candle went out, making the room completely dark.

Except it wasn't a breeze. It was warm and humid which meant it was someone's breath. Someone had blown the candle out. One good puff would have doused the flames.

So, somehow or other somebody had set up the lights to go out. Then with everyone distracted, that person had blown out the candles so the room would be completely dark. After that, no one would have known if they'd gotten out of their chair, because we'd all dropped hands at that point. Apparently Jez's admonition to not let go no matter what had fallen on deaf ears.

Anyone could have gotten out of their seat and bashed Jez on the head. Well, almost anyone. I was certain Lucas hadn't left my side. Ditto Rupert. He had clenched my hand tightly until the lights went on.

The question was, who made the lights go off in the first place? And how? If it had to be by remote, using a smartphone, as Rupert explained, who would have the know-how to hack the password? Did anyone?

Then another thought occurred to me. Bill had left his phone on the counter where anyone could have seen it. Had someone taken the opportunity to grab it? If so, they could have turned out the lights. Once they were back on and everyone was focused on Jez, they could have put the phone back. Yes, that made more sense. But who?

I tried to remember the order in which everyone entered the room. Jez had already been there when I walked in. Then the professor and Martin had arrived. I clearly remembered the professor's very loud complaints. Lavender had been right behind them. I replayed the evening in my head, watching as one-by-one the guests entered the room, until...

I sat bold upright in bed.

"It can't be."

"Wh—," Lucas mumbled.

"But it has to be. There's no other explanation." I jumped out of bed, grabbed my robe, and flung open the door. There was only one person who could have done it. I knew who the killer was.

#

I sailed down the hall dressed in nothing but pajamas and an unbelted robe. I hadn't even bothered to stop and put my bra on. I pounded on the door so hard it rattled in the frame. Somewhere in the back of my mind I registered how solid the door was and was impressed with myself.

The door swung open revealing Monica Carsley in a faded green dressing gown with a droopy hem and a ripped pocket. How many dressing gowns had she packed? She gave me what passed for a glare. "What do you want?"

"Who is it?" James snarled from inside the room.

"It's that Viola woman," Monica said.

"Does she know what time it is?"

"Of course I know what time it is." I pushed past her into the room and snapped on the overhead light. James was half out of bed. Fortunately for my sanity, he wore a t-shirt and a pair of sweat pants. It would have been incredibly awkward if he were one of those types who slept *au naturale*.

"What the blazes are you about?" he snapped. He eyes flashed dark and angry.

"Not a morning person, are you?" I gave him a smug smile. "Too, bad. Because I know who did it."

"What are you talking about?" Monica tugged the collar of her robe up around her neck. Her eyes had that deer-in-the-headlights look. I was a little worried she might pass out.

"I was trying to recall who could possibly have hit Jez during the séance. I thought at first it must be James. Sorry, James." I gave him an apologetic look. He shrugged as if to say "whatever." I turned back to Monica feeling triumphant. "There was only one person it could have been."

"Who?" she asked. Her hands were shaking a little.

"You." I pointed a finger straight at her. She let out a little squeak and stumbled backward a step. I continued. "It wasn't that hard to figure it out. It happened so quickly there's no way anyone seated even a couple of chairs away from Jez could have grabbed a weapon, hit her, hid the weapon, and got back in their seat before the lights came on. But you, you were sitting right next to her. You could have easily grabbed the candle stick, smacked her, and put it back, no one the wiser."

"That's ridiculous," she said, but all the color had drained from her face. She groped for the edge of the bed and sank down. "Just silly, really. I would never... I couldn't... James, tell her."

"Monica's a ninny," James assured me. "She'd never hurt a fly."

"Of course not," I agreed. "Not unless she was forced into it."

His eyes glittered coldly and his mouth formed a hard line. "What are you saying?"

"I'm saying that there's one person who could manipulate Monica into committing violence. You."

"That's ridiculous," he scoffed.

"Is it?" I crossed my arms. "Look at her. She's a mouse. Sorry, Monica."

She waved me off as if being called a mouse was a regular event.

"Why would I have my wife attack Jez? That's insane." His outrage seemed real, but there was such an aura of anger around him, I knew I was on the right track.

"Because you needed a distraction. And you needed to make sure that you were in the clear. You were afraid Jez had figured out the truth."

He sneered. "And what is the truth?"

"That you killed Jeffrey Blodgett."

Shéa MacLeod

Chapter 20
As Poirot Would Say

By that time several of the guests had gathered in the hall behind me. Probably I'd woken them up with my door banging and dramatics. Good. I could use an audience. Mostly because if the expression on James Carsley's face was anything to go by, I'd be a dead woman if it wasn't for the fact there were witnesses.

"We already went over this," he said as if I were stupid. "I admit, I meant to kill him. He deserved it for murdering my brother. But I didn't. Someone else got to him first."

"No." I shook my head. "You wanted us to *think* someone got to him first. It was actually really clever."

He crossed his arms as if to mimic me. "How so." There was an arrogant tilt to his head that made me want to wipe the smug smile right off his face.

"The fact is, you killed Blodgett right after I saw the two of you arguing. I don't know what set you off. Maybe you planned to kill him all along. Or maybe he goaded you with his lack of repentance. In any case, you strangled him. Squeezed his throat until he was dead." Carsley didn't move, didn't make a sound, so I continued. "You knew that if anyone found him dead, they'd know you did it. I'm sure I wasn't the only one who saw the two of you arguing. You knew about the secret passage from Robbie, didn't you?"

He shrugged. "What of it?"

"Robbie was fascinated with old buildings and secret passages and, according to the vicar, he spent a lot of time here at the manor. I'm betting he told you about this one. In a letter. An email. Who knows? But you knew exactly where it was. So, you dragged Blodgett's body across the library and hid it in the secret passage. Just in time, too, because Professor Huxton-Barrington was on her way to steal a first edition to fund her many plastic surgeries."

"Excuse me!" The professor's outraged voice came from behind me in the hall.

I turned around and eyed her coldly. "By the way, Professor, I suggest that book be returned to the library before you leave Wytham Manor. Otherwise I shall be forced to turn you over to the authorities. Understood?"

The professor blanched, but nodded. I returned to the matter at hand.

"You waited a couple hours, then returned to the library. You dragged the body back to the desk chair and stabbed Blodgett in the back with the letter opener you'd taken earlier. That way if anyone began to suspect you, you could admit to the stabbing. You knew, of course, that modern forensics would prove that the dagger hadn't killed him and you'd be in the clear."

"Great fairy tale. If you believe in that nonsense."

"I don't know," Lucas said lazily. "I think she might be on to something."

I was suddenly grateful Lucas was there. If looks could kill, James would have murdered me several minutes ago.

"Go on, Viola," Jez urged, moving into the doorway behind Lucas. "I want to know what happened next. Don't you all?"

There was a murmur of assent from the rest of the group. Apparently I had a captive audience.

"Your plan went off without a hitch. Like I said, it was very smart." I gave him an approving nod. "I'm certain that if it weren't for the flood, the police would have arrived and—while you may have been arrested early on—you would have been quickly cleared and on your way. Unfortunately, you were stuck here with the rest of us and Marilyn began hinting she knew who the killer was." I sighed. "Poor Marilyn. I highly doubt she knew anything at all, but Marilyn was one of those people who likes to stir the pot, if you know what I mean. You couldn't risk it. She had to die." I gave him a cool look. "You might as well admit it. The truth is as clear as the nose on your face." A delightful phrase I'd picked up reading too many Agatha Christie novels.

James was grinding his teeth, his jaw muscles flexing. Monica wept softly. "Oh, shut up, you old cow," he snarled, throwing a box of tissues at her. "You're the reason we're in this predicament."

"Don't blame Monica for your shortcomings," I said calmly, picking up the box which had tumbled to the floor. "It's not her fault you're a murderer." I handed her a tissue which she took with a wobbly smile of gratitude.

He snorted. "If she'd done her job—."

"You know Monica isn't a violent person. Forcing her into attacking Jez was pure stupidity. Sort of like killing Marilyn. If you hadn't left the tainted syringe in the disposal container, we might never have figured out how she died. But I'm guessing you were out of options. You got interrupted maybe."

"He was wandering around," James said, glaring at Rupert who stood in the doorway just behind Jez. "I had to get rid of it and couldn't have him catch me walking around with it. I was hoping no one would look in there and I'd have time to come back and get it. Stupid old bat should have kept her mouth shut."

"Once again, you thought you were in the clear. Then Jez suggested a séance and you freaked out again. What if one of the ghosts of your victims came through and pointed a finger at you?"

He snorted. "I don't believe in ghosts."

"Really?" I lifted an eyebrow. "Then why worry about a séance?"

"Because I thought I had another Marilyn on my hands!" he exploded. "I thought that stupid ghost hunter was just trying to use that mumbo jumbo to blackmail me."

"Hey!" Jez's tone was indignant. "It's not mumbo jumbo."

We all ignored her. James had gotten off the bed, but his whole frame was poised as if to bolt. I didn't know how he planned to get out since the exit was blocked by several people.

"You decided she had to die, too. Just like the others," I said, trying to keep my voice as soothing as possible. I didn't need him attacking anyone. "You knew the lights could be controlled by a phone, so when Bill left his on the counter, you grabbed it. Somehow, you convinced Monica to help you so that when you turned out the lights, everyone would be distracted. She could blow out the candle, then use the candlestick to hit Jez and kill her."

"I couldn't do it," Monica wailed. "I'm not a killer. Jez didn't do anything. How could I kill her?" She sobbed wildly, crumpling onto the bed.

"You're so bloody smart," James sneered. "But you couldn't stop me, could you? And you can't stop me now."

He moved so fast I was left standing there like an idiot with my mouth open. One minute he was poised as if for flight, and the next, he yanked Monica off the bed and held a knife to her throat. It was one of those folding pocket knives that was only just legal in the UK. But even such a small blade would be deadly if it nicked an artery.

"Now everyone move," he said. "Or I'll kill her."

Nobody moved. I think maybe they were in shock.

"Where are you going to go, James?" I asked. "Everything's flooded. You can't get out of here. And you can't kill us all."

I saw Lucas wince. Maybe that was the wrong thing to say. But James surprised me by throwing his head back and letting out a cackling bout of laughter.

"That's where you're wrong. The water's gone down. I was leaving in the morning anyway."

Lucas stepped toward him, but stopped as James pressed the knife harder against Monica's throat. A tiny spot of blood beaded against her pale skin.

"Don't be a hero," James said calmly. "You don't want her to die, do you?"

"Dear boy, there's no need for these amateur theatrics," the colonel said. He moved slowly into the room, leaning heavily on a cane.

"Shut up, old man. Nobody asked you."

The colonel gave Lucas a sideways look. Then Lucas grabbed the colonel's cane and threw it at James Carsley's head. James ducked, yanking his knife hand away from Monica who tumbled to the floor with a shriek.

With Monica out of the way, Lucas charged toward James. James's gaze caught mine and I knew what he planned to do. I opened my mouth, but it was too late.

James Carsley threw himself through the glass window to the flagstones below. Everyone froze for a moment, then I rushed toward the window. Lucas grabbed me before I reached it.

"Don't look." His voice was gruff. "You don't want to see it. I promise."

"Is he...?"

"Bloody hell!" an angry voice shouted from below. "I broke my bloody leg!"

Lucas gave me a look. "Compound fracture. It's pretty disgusting."

I made a face and backed away from the window. He was right. I definitely didn't want to see that.

Shéa MacLeod

Chapter 21
Return to Chipping Poggs

The police arrived a few hours later just as the sun peeked above the horizon, painting the landscape in pinks and golds. For the first time in days there was no rain, just an endless stretch of robin's egg blue sky.

An ambulance followed hot on the heels of the police, and James was arrested, handcuffed, and hauled off to the nearest hospital. Lucas and the Colonel had made a tourniquet to stop the bleeding, but the medics had to inject him with a sedative because he wouldn't stop screaming and cursing.

The hotel had become a crime scene, so the police took statements from everyone and then let the locals—like Lavender who lived in London, and the Huxton-Barringtons who were from Oxford—go home. Jez, Lucas, and I had to relocate to an inn at a nearby village. Colonel Frampton joined us, declaring that he was still on holiday and didn't intend to finish it early. Personally, I thought he was a lonely man looking for some company. Which was fine with me. He could be an arrogant jerk sometimes, but he was all right.

We were sitting around a table in the pub next door to our new inn. It was a modern chain establishment lacking the charm of the Beast and Bauble. Still, the food was good and the drinks cheap.

"You know." I turned to the colonel who was sipping a pint of dark ale. "This morning was the first time I saw you use a cane."

He grinned, his moustache lifting like the wings of a butterfly. "Despite my advanced age, I don't require use of a cane. I only keep it around for walks in the woods. It comes in handy as a walking stick and to bash down encroaching branches and such. I figured it might come in handy. And who would notice an old man leaning on a cane?" He waggled his thick eyebrows and I laughed.

"I guess Lucas did."

"What I want to know is did James come to Chipping Poggs planning to kill Blodgett?" Jez said. "And, if so, how did he know Blodgett would be there?"

"I talked to the detective in charge," Colonel Frampton said. "Carsley claims he only went to Chipping Poggs to honor the tenth anniversary of his brother's disappearance. Perhaps he needed closure. Who knows? But he claims that he never expected to run into Blodgett, nor had he planned to kill the man."

"I find that unlikely," I said drily. "That whole thing took some planning."

"Poor Mrs. Carsley." The colonel shook his head. "It's her I feel sorry for. She is the one who knocked at the séance. She was trying to alert us to her husband's evil doing. Or so she claims."

Now there was some new information. I guess it hadn't been a ghost, after all. "She could have been a little more obvious about it instead of leaving us to figure out some knocking nonsense. A note would have been nice."

"I wonder what will happen to her," Jez said. "I mean, okay, she hit me, but he kind of forced her into it."

"I'm guessing that since we all witnessed his treatment of her, the judge will be lenient," Lucas said. "Technically she's an accomplice. If not before the fact, then certainly after. But she'll probably get a few months for obstruction or something and be out before you know it."

I felt sorry for Monica, but I wasn't sure a few months was enough punishment for what she'd done. Then again, she was married to a man who made her life hell, so maybe she'd been punished plenty already.

"Well, I'm off to bed," the colonel declared, rising from the table. "I've an early start tomorrow."

"Where are you off to?" I asked.

He waggled his eyebrows. "A sixties plus walking tour of the French countryside. Rumor has it the ladies will far outnumber the gentlemen."

"Why, you sly dog," I laughed.

He chortled with glee, tipped an imaginary hat, and only staggered slightly as he strolled out of the pub and into the cool evening air. Oddly, I'd kind of miss him.

"How about you?" Lucas asked Jez. "What are your plans?"

"Well, I haven't finished my investigations of St. Oswin's. I talked to Rupert today, and he said the police have released the manor and I can go back tomorrow."

"You're returning to Chipping Poggs?" I asked, surprised she'd want to go back to the scene of so much death. No to mention her own head bashing.

She grinned. "You bet. Can you imagine how many ghosts are wandering around Wytham Manor now?"

It was late when she finally left, but Lucas and I stayed at the pub chatting over our drinks about nothing in particular. It was a relief to be away from murder and mayhem, but things were still a little strained between us.

"I owe you an apology."

I glanced up at him, startled. "What?"

He took my hand, rubbing his thumb gently across the back of it, drawing lazy little circles. "I'm sorry I didn't tell you about my family sooner. I should have. It's just…it's very difficult and awkward."

"I'm your girlfriend," I pointed out. "What's the point of having me in your life if you can't share difficult stuff with me?"

He gave me a wry smile. "True."

"And you don't have to point out the irony of me being frustrated over lack of communication since it took me months to get around to admitting we were a thing."

He laughed. "A thing?"

"You know what I mean."

He gave me a long, meaningful look that heated my blood. Man, it was warm in the pub all of a sudden.

"Truth is," he said, "my family dynamics are a little strange."

"You haven't met my mother yet, have you?"

"No, actually."

"When you do, believe me, you will experience the meaning of strange. She knows you and I are together, yet she insists on trying to play matchmaker. It's embarrassing."

"That's not so bad."

I lifted an eyebrow. "You want her to marry me off to a wine maker from France?"

He chuckled. "That would, indeed, be awkward, since I've no intention of letting you go."

That gave me the warm fuzzies. "How awkward can your family be?"

He sighed heavily. "Both my parents are Jewish. My mother is from Israel, and my father from Italy."

"Right. So?"

"So, they're not pleased that I don't practice the religion or keep kosher."

I tilted my head thoughtfully. "I can understand that. I don't come from a particularly religious family, but I know those who do. Breaking from family tradition is always difficult."

"Indeed. There have been many arguments over it. And over the fact I choose to live in America instead of Israel near my parents and brother."

"Okay, but why wouldn't you tell me this? I'd have understood."

He rubbed his jaw. "The last time we spoke, I told my mother about you."

My eyes widened. By the tone of his voice I could tell it hadn't gone well. "Oh, dear."

"Exactly. She didn't take it well, me dating a "gentile." We had bit of an, ah, argument."

"Over me?"

He squeezed my hand. "I love you, Viola. And I don't care how upset my mother is over it, you're the woman I want to be with."

I blinked. He'd argued with his mother over me? "I love you, too."

"I didn't want to talk about it because…well, I didn't want to upset you. Forgive me?"

"Of course. Although family get togethers are going to be awkward."

#

I lay awake again that night, staring at the shadows dancing across the ceiling and listening to Lucas snore. Tomorrow we were headed to London where we'd catch a flight back to Oregon. There'd been a little too much excitement in Chipping Poggs. I couldn't wait to get home to my calm, normal life in Astoria.

Normal? I frowned, remembering all the police investigations I'd gotten wrapped up in over the past few months. Well, maybe normal was relative, but at least there wouldn't be any ghosts.

The End

A Note from Shéa

Thank you for reading. If you enjoyed this book, I'd appreciate it if you'd help others find it so they can enjoy it too.

- Lend it: This e-book is lending-enabled, so feel free to share it with your friends, readers' groups, and discussion boards.

- Review it: Let other potential readers know what you liked or didn't like about the story.

Book updates can be found at www.sheamacleod.com

Shéa MacLeod

About Shéa MacLeod

Shéa MacLeod is the author of the bestselling paranormal series, Sunwalker Saga, as well as the award nominated cozy mystery series Viola Roberts Cozy Mysteries. She has dreamed of writing novels since before she could hold a crayon. She totally blames her mother.

She resides in the leafy green hills outside Portland, Oregon where she indulges in her fondness for strong coffee, Ancient Aliens reruns, lemon curd, and dragons. She can usually be found at her desk dreaming of ways to kill people (or vampires). Fictionally speaking, of course.

Shéa MacLeod

Other Books by Shéa MacLeod

<u>Viola Roberts Cozy Mysteries</u>
The Corpse in the Cabana
The Stiff in the Study
The Poison in the Pudding
The Body in the Bathtub
The Venom in the Valentine
The Remains in the Rectory
The Death in the Drink

<u>Notting Hill Diaries</u>
To Kiss a Prince
Kissing Frogs
Kiss Me, Chloe
Kiss Me, Stupid
Kissing Mr. Darcy

<u>Cupcake Goddess Novelettes</u>
Be Careful What You Wish For
Nothing Tastes As Good
Soulfully Sweet
A Stich in Time

<u>Dragon Wars</u>
Dragon Warrior
Dragon Lord
Dragon Goddess
Green Witch

<u>Lady Rample</u>
Lady Rample Steps Out
Lady Rample Spies a Clue
Lady Rample and the Silver Screen
Lady Rample and the Ghost of Christmas Past
Lady Rample and Cupid's Kiss
Lady Rample and the Mysterious Mr. Singh

<u>Sunwalker Saga: Soulshifter Trilogy</u>
Fearless
Haunted
Soulshifter

<u>Witchblood Mysteries</u>
<u>Coming Soon</u>
Spells and Sigils
Death and Demons
Mists and Magic
Dreams and Danger

<u>Omicron ZX</u>
Omicron Zed-X: Omicron ZX prequel Novellette

A Rage of Angel

Printed in Dunstable, United Kingdom